CAPTURED

BY THE

Phantom

THE PHANTOM SERIES, BOOK THREE

JENNIFER DESCHANEL

Captured by the Phantom
Jennifer Deschanel

2nd Edition -- ALL RIGHTS RESERVED
Cover Art: Dar Albert of Wicked Smart Designs
Print Formatting: Nina Pierce of Seaside Publications

ISBN: 9781794059665

LOUIS
BEVERLY
Romance
SINCE 1968

DEDICATION

For my mother, Kathy,
a true heroine.

With memory set smarting like a reopened wound, a man's past is not simply a dead history, an outworn preparation of the present: it is not a repented error shaken loose from life: it is a still quivering part of himself, bringing shudders and bitter flavours and the tinglings of a merited shame.

~George Eliot

ONE

It was his birthday, and the Vicomte de Chagny was thinking of ways to kill himself.

The toast ended. He raised his glass in half-hearted acknowledgment before wanting to rip the lingering hurrahs out of his ears. The music resumed, and men in formal black trousers, waistcoats, and white ties took to swirling white clad maids across the highly polished marble. Not that he cared. Eyes pulled so wide he swore they would pop, André Thaddeus Marie, the Vicomte de Chagny, regarded in stupid horror the surreal man plundering his way across the room.

André's hand tightened around the champagne flute. He eyed the mantle to his side. One slight rap would be all it would take. He could shatter the glass and thrust the makeshift blade dead center of his chest. Death would be swift, and he wouldn't have to face what was an inevitability about to ruin his sixteenth birthday. The man locked sights on him, instantly clamming André's brow. This was a sick champagne-induced hallucination. He turned to the circle gathering around him.

1

"So are we to assume music is in your future, André?"

André smiled at his godfather, Jules Legard. He surveyed the room before replying. Legard didn't seem concerned, and he was head of Chagny security. His godfather's question was lighthearted. That was good though. He hadn't noticed anything was amiss. Life could move on as usual for a few more seconds.

"I'm afraid I don't have a talent for music," André replied, forcing charisma to shine like the diamonds in his cuffs.

He learned that trick from his diva mother. Always remain calm when eyes were upon you. But where did those eyes go? A bead of sweat trickled down the back of his neck. It felt like an invisible spider he couldn't crush. The massive mirrored wall to his side reflected the room as he searched it. Nothing seemed off. He turned from his reflection and despite his ill ease, he nodded kindly at a blushing young maiden making doe eyes in his direction—*that* useful trick he learned from his father. Raoul Jean-Paul Marie, the Comte de Chagny, charmed the ladies and always permitted them time—even if a serpent was poised to strike.

"What cares have I for music?" André's laugh was rusty. "Notes are like thousands of annoying ants tromping off to ruin a picnic." Gesturing with his drink, he pointed one finger sharply at his godfather. "Don't you dare say I take after my mother."

"You should watch your tongue, Vicomte de Chagny, lest I make you prove what an accomplished baritone you truly are."

With a quick survey of the room to judge how much time he had before all hell cracked open, André flashed a smile at his mother's response then dropped it like a handful of lead. She lifted her glass in a toast and offered him a peck on his cheek before leaving him alone on her bell-like laughter with the men gathered around him.

Thank God she headed in the opposite direction. No need for her to witness them all burning alive.

"He has a double first in mathematics and classics, Jules. I dare say if he continues this strong he can do whatever he wishes."

André rocked forward as father's hand slapped his back as

2

hard as his praise had done. Too bad it didn't knock him senseless. "While revisiting Paris has been a delight, all I wish to do is return to Chagny in time to mount my stallion for the hunting season."

A voice from behind him slid into his ears and made his toes curl. "There are finer things to mount in life, Monsieur le Vicomte. But then again rumor has it you've already mastered the art of dipping your swell into the rumps of fine young maids. I am, oh so proud."

André's lips turned into a tight line. This was no hallucination. This was an absolute nightmare. He glanced between the stone-hard stares of Legard and his father before inching around to face the rough, travel haggard man. Locking his eyes back on his father, André saw him clutch his champagne flute so tightly it was a miracle it didn't shatter. Legard's face was crimson.

"André, attend your mother." His father's voice was low. Too low.

Unwilling to protest and utterly shocked to be staring at Loup, André made a hasty retreat. Glancing over his shoulder, André watched as the champagne flute finally exploded as his father slammed it down on the sideboard.

"My library. Now," the comte demanded of the bounty hunter, shaking his hand free of champagne.

Swallowing hard, André watched them storm from the ballroom. He glared remorsefully at his champagne glass. A birthday death would have been much better than this.

As the strains of the latest waltz swirled in the distance, Raoul focused on the fury rushing blood into his ears. Pacing around the library, he made several passes before stopping to glare out the floor to ceiling window. The reflection that stared back at him, dim and ghost-like, served him an extra dose of disgust. Behind him, Loup reclined casually on a settee; an arm slung over its back as he gradually drained a champagne flute.

"A year." Raoul spun from the reflection and stormed across the room. "I don't hear from you in a year, and now you show up unannounced at my son's celebration?"

"How sweet. You missed me."

Loup quaffed his champagne and propped a muddy boot on the seat. Raoul was usually a calm man, but this time he allowed himself to feel his outrage to the fullest.

"You perpetual drunkard!" With one swipe of his arm, Raoul ripped the glass from Loup's grasp and flung it into the fireplace. The delicate crystal shattered, firing glass back at his feet.

Loup narrowed his eyes. "Temper, temper."

"Have you forgotten how to send word?" Legard interrupted.

Raoul eyed Legard before scrubbing ramming a finger beneath this tie and yanking down. The bow fell free, but it did nothing to loosen the invisible noose around his neck. Minutes ago he was enjoying a delightful evening, and now the past stalked him like a hungry lioness.

"Where the hell have you been?" he interjected sharply.

Loup drew a line between the two of them with his look before he studied his cuticles. "Sightseeing. I spent some time in a room with high security."

"You were in prison?" Legard yelled, arms akimbo.

"Where do you think I've been?" Loup stood, more pompous than a king at court. "You can stand here and look stupid, or I can tell you what I know and leave you to your petty evening."

Raoul jerked one hand to the ceiling and let it slap to his side. This would prove an interesting tale. The tension was drawn as tight as a bowstring, and before it snapped, Raoul glanced to Legard. Maybe looking at him would keep him from murder right now.

"Germany," Loup continued. "I had a mighty fine tryst with a Baron's daughter. Devilish shag that one."

Acid inched up Raoul's throat.

"After he threw me in prison, I learned of a monastery he was fond of in a small village. I decided to cut my sentence short and visit the village. I was going to burn the church as a thank-you for the kind accommodation he paid me over the last year but the organ, you see, was far too extraordinary." "If you so much as laid a hand on a house of God—" Raoul pinched the bridge of his nose. If he only he could turn back time and never have tangled his life with this cur. "Very fascinating carvings on the organ cabinet. The dome of the Opera Garnier and the blackened masks caught my eye." "What are you telling me?" Raoul snapped.

"I believe The Phantom of the Opera is sequestered near a monastery in Baden-Württemburg Germany close to the Austrian border." Raoul sorted through a full year of information. Perplexed, he shook his head. "Baden-Württemburg? Last, the Persian indicated we should keep to the Royal Opera in Sweden. The Phantom was likely there."

"Yes, and the opera houses in Salzburg, Rome, Barcelona, Copenhagen..." Loup dragged air over his tongue. "Your opera houses are dead ends and your Persian as helpful as gout. He's in Germany I assure you."

"But you said you believe?" Legard interrupted. "You're uncertain?"

The bounty hunter shrugged.

Raoul plowed a hand through his hair as he walked to his desk. He grabbed a clump as if to dig into his brain. Lowering himself into his seat, he folded his hands before his mouth like a prayerful priest. For years he pursued Erik for the crimes he committed at the Opera Garnier. Endless, hellish years of watching Christine vacillate between locking the Phantom away forever and her steadfast devotion to her former tutor. Her Angel of Music! Now—it could be all at its end. Raoul rattled his thoughts into order. "We should check with the Persian again before moving this to Germany."

"Oh, bloody hell you're a blithering imbecile!" Loup shouted. "That Persian is leading you in circles on purpose. His dark ass would be twitching at the opposite end of a guillotine if left to me. Any fool can see he has some allegiance to your Phantom. I'm getting a delightful trek around the world on your purse string, but would rather have my balls squeezed between a tight quim instead of touring one opera house after the next. It's not challenging." He rapped his head with a finger. The motion made his beady eyes seem to spin in their sockets. "You must think like a fugitive, not a gentleman. You should know by now opera houses are dead ends."

"I'm not about to upend innocent villages or disturb a monastery without absolute confirmation the Phantom is there," Raoul said.

"All well and good, but I'm not about to do a damn thing without my pocket padded. Where's my money?"

Raoul hardened his gaze. "You disappear for a year, challenge who I elect to question and then have the audacity to demand my purse?"

"That was the arrangement. I don't hunt for free."

"The arrangement included proof." Raoul's shout bounced off the mosaic floor, nearly cracking the tiles. "You're not getting a dime from me. God's blood, you can't even bring in Anna Barret!"

The way Loup's tongue flicked out at the mention of Erik's companion tightened Raoul's neck. Loup pressed his palms against the worn wood of the desk and leaned in close. The man's breath was vile as his morals. It curled his lip.

"It's your misfortune that Anna was involved in assisting the Phantom escape his crimes, Monsieur le Comte. She's a cunning little wench, but I'll find her." Loup laughed. "Anna's capture for the murder of that Duke's heir is gold. Only word of her death may stem the search in the good Duke's eye, but she is *my* commodity, and I want her. I don't see you growing a spine to track them. Frankly, I don't see you doing much of anything requiring backbone." Loup's head lolled to the side with a droll expression as he regarded Raoul. He lifted a hand and rippled his fingers toward his palm. "Coat my hand, and I'll be on my way. I'm mostly positive they're in Baden."

"Mostly isn't good enough."

"Monsieur le Comte is correct," Legard agreed. Raoul flicked his gaze in his direction. About time he spoke up. "I'll not have Chagny involved in disrupting the peace. We need proof."

6

Loup shoved off the desk. "What proof do you need? I saw the organ. The village was as poor as they come. Where would they get one if not built by your musical genius? Why would monks give a fig about Parisian opera?"

"That Baron held it in esteem; he could have gifted the organ. And I've known several creative Brothers," Raoul said.

"Talented enough to decorate it with *black* masks? I don't recall any mentioned in the Bible. God, you're pathetically stupid."

"If you're so confident he was in the village then why didn't you bring him here?" Legard challenged.

Loup smiled like a cat that had swallowed a canary. "I had to make a hasty retreat. Seems a prayer candle tipped over."

"*For the love of God*! You burned down a monastery's church?" Raoul dug into his brain again, feeling strands of hair brake off in his grip. His voice lifted. "I'll make amends to the village later, as soon as we have the Phantom in our grasp. I simply can't think of that now. Erik is living a normal life in the German countryside as if he never abducted Christine, never killed the managers of the Garnier, and never burned down a carriage house. After all he did to Paris and Christine... after killing *my brother*, how dare that man live without a conscience!" His fist hit his desk turning his signet into a gavel. Raoul glanced from Loup to address Legard. "We need to know for sure if he is in Germany. Go to the *Rue de Rivoli*. Wake the Persian if you must; this can't wait. Ask him directly about these opera houses. If anyone knows Erik's wandering ways, he does." Legard nodded while Loup rolled his eyes. Raoul jerked his head in his direction. "If you have better means to back up your suspicions then speak them now." He spoke to Legard again. "Find out what you can, then you," he pinned Loup with his look, "will return to Germany and not return without an end to this manhunt."

Spit slid down the wood. Loup watched it slime the library door thinking he had better things to make wet than polished wood.

The comte dare shout orders at him? Chagny owed him money, and he knew exactly where to get it. It would just be a matter of finding her alone. But later. Right now his gut needed liquor and his loins a good shag. It trumped any necessity to locate the Comtesse de Chagny and her purse, but to his good fortune, he didn't have to. Loup smirked as the beauty rounded the corner. Her delicate hand fluttered at the base of her throat as she regarded the floor. She was such a pathetic target. Wiping the spittle from his lips, Loup pressed a long leg against a marble column and leaned back against it.

"Comtesse de Chagny. Miss me?" Like a deer before the bow of a hunter, she froze. He sneered. "Come now. Don't look so shocked. You knew I'd return. We have a deal, remember?"

All good humor faded from her face. Her porcelain skin blanched. Fine lines spread across its flawless perfection, aging her instantly. Loup loved how easy she was to startle. So unlike Anna.

"What are you doing here?" she gasped. "You've not found Erik, have you?"

What, no warm welcome? "I might have. Your husband is eager to bring him in but reluctant to pay me. One of you must, or someone won't be happy."

Loup pushed off the column and swaggered toward her. The comtesse was always a meek thing, the perfect toy to which to amuse himself until he had Anna back in his grip. Nothing compared to that feisty piece of thatch. His skills as a hunter were unrivaled. He always got what he wanted in the blink of an eye— except Anna. The blasted woman had become his prize game, and the idea of giving up his favorite target to anyone raised his temper. He would prevail somehow and savor every moment of victory while his pockets filled with money, and his swell with Anna's tight sex.

He trailed a gritty finger down Christine's elegant arm and walked behind her admiring her shape and size.

"It would be amusing to see what would happen if I spilled that secret I've been keeping all these years of your love for the Phantom. It might be more fun than the money you're paying me to keep silent about it. The scandal would level Chagny to rubble. Poor André would lose so much, now, wouldn't he?" Loup rested his chin on her shoulder and wiggled his palms before her. "I believe I know where Erik is and your husband is desperate for me to capture him. If you still want me to keep your marriage the happy little lie, it is—pay up!" A lewd chuckle grew deep in his throat. He loved when women trembled. The need between his legs grew great, tightening his trousers to discomfort. Though it was an alluring thought to shove her against the column and his cock up inside her, he was in the mood for a more combative shag.

"You know how to fill my bags with the money."

Lightly shoving her away, Loup spun on his heal and headed down the hall, his hands dangling before him like a puppeteer working the strings of a marionette. The gentle tune of *Alouette* skipped beside him down the corridor.

Christine refused to turn until that tune faded. Her worst nightmare danced in the hall of her home and it made the air around her icy. Her heartbeat ticked fearfully making it near impossible to catch her breath. When she did turn, a gasp leaped from her mouth.

"André, I didn't see you." She looked beyond him. Loup had disappeared. It was little comfort.

"I didn't mean to startle you, *Maman*."

Christine smoothed the lines of her gown and tapped her cheeks to pink them. Years of stage training came into play as she covered her nerves flawlessly. "All is well, André. I was merely seeking your father. Return to your party. We'll speak later."

Her son didn't move. A knot tightened around her neck as she watched him extend a leg and jut his hip. *So like his father.*

"Why is Loup here?" he asked. "He usually surfaces like a bad potato, but he's been gone for quite some time. I thought perhaps for good at last." André jabbed a finger in the direction Loup disappeared making Christine bit her tongue. He was, indeed, too much like his father. "That man's despicable behavior and morals is not something I appreciate associated with my family—despite father's desires. Does he have word on the Phantom and Mademoiselle Barret?"

The hall might as well have been a stage, but she the only actor. André had a knack for speaking his mind as he saw fit, and had a way of reading her that was unnatural for a son. She had to give her best performance yet. She tapped his arm.

"I have no idea why he has returned. I'll speak to your father of it, André. Go, return to your guests."

She kissed him on his cheek hoping that icy sensation she felt inside didn't make her lips cold and betray her to her son. Praying her placation worked she hastened past him and the library door and forgot all about Raoul. Air is what she needed, and this time she dared not turn around lest her son read the cheat on her face.

Two

He read the same sentence four times. Glancing over the book's rim, he let it fall lax between two fingers. Paris was supposed to equal solitude and culture for him; that was a load of malarkey the longer the pounding on his door persisted. Slapping his book on his side table, Vahid scowled toward the door then at the clock mercilessly ticking away at the unheard of hour.

"I'm coming! There's little need to break down my door!"

If he could get away with assault, he'd fling open the door and wring the neck of whoever pounded apart his peace. The rapping continued raising his ire with every step he took across his elaborate Persian carpet. As the former daroga, chief of police to Persia's Sultana, privacy was luxury he had come to enjoy, having had little of it during his time in Persia. Being disturbed regardless of the hour wasn't something he found pleasant unless a harem of virgins were hammering their way into his apartments. That would be the only acceptable reason for the unrelenting knocking. Yanking open the door, the face greeting him skewed his brow.

"For all Allah has in Paradise, what do *you* want?"

"Daroga, may I have a word?" Legard politely bowed and removed his hat as if being cordial was going to change Vahid's mood.

"No, you may not. Go away." Vahid leaned all his weight against the door in an attempted to shut it, but his uninvited guest shoved a boot between the jambs and forced his way into the modest flat. Vahid watched with growing impatience as Legard peeled off his gloves and placed them inside his hat.

"You're not going to offer me a drink?" Legard asked.

"I have hemlock."

Legard smiled. It was wry, skewing Vahid's face even more. He knew the reasons the former Paris investigator was here. It made him wish to combust like the strike of a match. "Inspector, leave my home you're not welcome here."

"When I'm on business my position is welcome anywhere. You should know that."

A sound of utter disgust burst out his mouth. It was pointless to argue; after all, Legard was already in his apartment. Vahid searched the room. *Where did I leave my drink?*

"Tell me, Daroga," Legard helped himself to a seat in an overstuffed chair. "These opera houses you keep suggesting? Any others you might have in mind? Hamburg perhaps? Shall we look for him there?"

Him. Vahid stopped mid-search. There it was again. The reason for these blasted unannounced meetings. He found his aperitif on his sideboard and downed it in one massive gulp. Vahid pressed a finger to the center of his chest and the burn sliding down his throat. He was getting too old for this. Legard had become his own Phantom, popping in and out of his life whenever Chagny needed information or hit a wall. He cursed himself under his breath as he poured a second drink. He should never have allowed Chagny to question him years ago in Lyon. Blissful ignorance should have been the way to go so he could have carried on with his life and not permitted his foolish curiosity over Erik to resurface.

"Do you have anything to say to me, Daroga?"

"Let me think a moment. Yes, go away."

"You know you can't hinder an investigation you're involved in."

Vahid's drink splashed over the rim of his glass to coat his hand as he spat his second swig out back into the glass. "Involved in? I have nothing to do with this! Deal with the investigation on your own, you incompetent, measly, old fool and leave me out of it."

"You *are* involved. We expect you to be—"

"—the eyes and ears for Chagny. Well aware, Monsieur. I suddenly feel blind and deaf in my old age."

The liquor churned within him along with the reality that keeping Erik out of his life was an impossibility. He, unlike most, had known his secrets for years. Shaking his drink off of his wrist, he looked at Legard. Just the sight of him made his nostrils flare. Vahid was aware Erik had faked his death years ago and never killed Philippe de Chagny, but he wasn't about to tell Legard that. Erik may have attempted to kill the former comte in the distant past, but the man's ultimate demise was not at the monster's hands. There was no proof. Regardless, Vahid made it a point to stay away from Erik when he did resurrect himself. He had no idea where Erik was. If Legard had any sense about him, he'd understand that logic would deem the monster would hide in the bowels of theaters like he always did. History tends to repeat, after all.

Vahid scowled. *Far be it from me to inform Chagny that the entire idea of Erik's faked death was Philippe de Chagny's, to begin with.* He swallowed a snort and swirled the drink in his glass. Maybe it would drown his thoughts. "Why you keep pestering me I'll never know. Not once—once," he shouted, "has Erik made contact with me. Yet here you are at my door again like a dog sniffing for a bone."

He shook his head as if to rattle the entire affair back into its proper place. Back then Erik's temper was explosive. Shamed and shunned in the most humiliating ways caused his old comrade to be unpredictable and Vahid had wanted nothing to do with him. Swore Erik out of his life forever, but unfortunately, he was a weak man—at least when it came to the ties he had to Erik.

Not this time. He was through.

Tossing the drink down on a side table so suddenly it wobbled and spun, he headed for the door and yanked it open. "Get out. I'll answer no more of your questions."

"Germany, Daroga, don't make me arrest you."

Vahid slammed the door shut making a mirror rattle on the wall. "Fine! Germany! Hell, no! For the last and final time, I'll tell you, not a chance!"

Legard rose, waving his hat in the air between them. "Then sending Loup back there to uncover what he found in a monastery in Baden-Württemburg is useless? It appears your opera houses are wild chases, Daroga."

"Then get off your damn high horse and out of my life."

Legard escalated the conversation to a shouting match. "By God, help us don't hinder us! The evidence is there. If Germany comes up empty then where do you suggest we look? And no opera houses. I grow weary of this game."

"He wouldn't be in Germany. He hates Germany always had. When will that get through to you?"

"Then *where,* Daroga? You know him better than most."

"Perhaps up your ass?"

A chilling silence followed the stalemate. "Thank you, for your time, Daroga. As always it was charming."

"Go drink from the river."

Tipping his hat, Legard stepped through the door that was being impatiently held open. "Delightful to see you again, too. Should you remember anything or decide you have information to assist us—"

"I'll be certain to jump naked into a scorpion's nest." Vahid flicked his wrist and slammed the door hard in Legard's face.

Once the crack stopped echoing in his apartments, Vahid retrieved his abandoned drink and sank into his armchair, sullen and bitter that a lovely evening had to end this way. There would be no finishing that book now. Glancing out the window, he watched Legard mount his horse and ride off toward the Tuileries.

Chagny was absolutely obsessed. When would they learn he was not going to give them an ounce of information even if he had it? If Chagny poured half their efforts into mopping up the crime riddling Paris, the streets would be so clean one could eat off of them.

"Germany." Vahid snorted. "Why would he be in Germany?" His brooding matched the falling night. Once Erik influenced one's life he remained an all too vivid part of it. The stories Vahid had heard about him in years rolled like wild dice in his head. But were they stories, or more rumor and legend? Erik was all too real to Raoul de Chagny that much was certain. The daroga sniffed his glass. All too real to him as well. He'd not set eyes on Erik years. Not since a brief encounter at a train station in some town whose name he'd long forgotten. Beyond that, the tales he remembered of Erik recalled a broken man; reclusive and scorned, wallowing in solitude beneath an opera house convinced the world would love without him.

But Erik *had* murdered again, that was one tale he couldn't ignore. The monster's deadly past, prevalent in Persia, seemed to haunt him still. Yet a paid political assassin was different. Or was it? Erik could have been such a remarkable man, capable of such glory and good. If only he had never laid eyes on Christine Daaé. Then he would never have known how much it could hurt to love and none of this would have ever happened.

Staring out the window only reflected Vahid's somber mood at him. He knew sides of Erik no one did, in particular, the side capable of being a great man with great love. He couldn't believe the images being painted for him by this pursuit. He tried desperately to put the thoughts out of his head, but he couldn't help but wonder about a long-lost chapter in his life.

"Baden-Württenburg," he whispered into his drink.

THREE

The frost on the window glinted in the early dawn light, blinding Erik to seeing anything but brilliant white. Nonetheless, he stared through the cottage's modest window and toward the direction of the monastery.

The charred wood had been hauled away, and the fire-scarred stones cleansed, but still, the stench of acrid smoke lingered in the air. It would be months until the pillar of the village rose again to shelter its flock. For now, the monastery's church wafted its untimely fate on a gentle breeze, and the persistent scent crept through a crack in the windowpane. Clasping his hands behind his back, Erik stood there, back ridged and mind tumbling over the idea that nothing in life was simple, least of all the unresolved mystery of why a fire would ever touch such an innocent place. Not to mention why a man such as him—a certain sinner—would be forgiven his past and given a peaceful, nondescript life in a German monastery.

"For someone who isn't a man of God, you've been down to the church more in these last few weeks than in all the years I've known you."

Erik turned and coolly regarded the monk sitting contentedly, and a touch arrogantly, in his chair by the morning fire. Erik preferred to dismiss socializing and had learned to put up with Brother Lukas' ever-persistent need to mention his lack of faith. Erik was satisfied with the same eerie solitude and beliefs that had always been his companion. He wasn't about to soul-search and change them. Still, Brother Lukas had put up a good fight for his salvation over the years so Erik couldn't blame him for trying. What Erik could do without, however, was the monk looking so smug in his favorite chair.

"Should you not be in private prayer before Lauds instead of bothering me?" Erik half-jokingly rumbled. Truth be told, didn't mind the monk's early morning company and did his best not to let that be known. "Being your personal cause for redemption is getting stale." Beneath his mask, he lifted a brow Brother Lukas couldn't see. The only thing he could see was the curl to Erik's lip that betrayed his jest.

"Personal causes aren't old, you are." Brother Lukas said nodding toward the window. "You shouldn't be sulking over a lost organ, Erik. Everything happens by God's design."

"I never believed in your God, and I dare say I am a better designer."

The monk chuckled, prompting Erik to smile. He turned back toward the frosted window and the ice crystals shimmering in the light. A master architect in addition to a brilliant maestro, Erik had crafted his way through this new, quiet life of his. The monastery brought him a place to call home, and a community of which to be a part. Brother Lukas had spent his afternoons in the carpentry shop, silently praying and tending to repairs for the monastery and church—until Erik arrived and took over, insisting that not even Christ was a better carpenter than he. So for the home and the simple things to occupy his time, Erik was thankful. Not that he'd wear that on his sleeve.

"Erik doesn't sulk; he broods," Anna replied.

Erik looked across the modest kitchen they had all gathered in and cocked his head at the petite woman seeing to his morning meal. The dawn attempting to peer through the window caught her hair, making it glimmer like a copper kettle peppered silver. The light trapped there drew him from the window like a macabre hummingbird to nectar. He slid behind her, walking his extraordinarily long fingers up her spine. The mask he wore spared the world all but his lips allowing him to gently touch that spot on her neck that he knew always made her knees soften.

"You may brood over a lost organ yet one side of you certainly has no problems with inspiration." Brother Lukas stopped worshiping the fire and tilted his head in Erik's direction.

"Consider it the least your fine God could do for me." Erik passed a hand over his mask. "I would offer to teach you the art of seduction, but I feel it would be lost on you."

"The art of seduction?" A cold blast of air swirled through a side door and around a grinning youth appearing in the doorway. He rippled his fingers through his hair building upon his roguish appearance before leaning his elbow on the doorframe. He shrugged his eyebrows. "Don't stop such conversation on my behalf. I assure you my curiosity is peaked."

Erik glowered. "Philippe, it is an ungodly hour. You never rise early. What are you doing roaming about?"

His son folded his arms and strolled into the kitchen. Unusually tall for fifteen, he dwarfed his mother as he passed. He yanked at the strip of leather holding his shoulder-length, brown hair in a neat queue, adjusted it, and tied it again. The brow he lifted accented eyes the color of a stormy Caribbean sea.

"I was looking for something." He rubbed the back of his neck.

"Looking for what?" Erik countered.

"Something I lost."

"Elaborate."

He didn't have to. The missing item tore through the door behind him, squealing gleefully at her freedom. The whorl of honey curls burst into the kitchen, her laughs a vibrant upheaval to the peace of any monastery. Her bare feet and the hem of her nightdress were hopelessly covered in cobwebs and dust. Her ever-present violin and bow were, as usual, clutched tightly in one hand. No-one understood why she carried the silent instrument; she didn't know how to play it. It was her security and went unquestioned. Slamming a hug into Erik's leg, she tilted her head as far back as she could and flashed a mischievous grin. The pungent, mildewed aroma hovering around her, reminiscent of Erik's years living in the cellars of the Opera Garnier, caused him to shoot a hot look to his son. Exactly where had his daughter been playing?

"*Philippe Georges Marie.*" A protective growl grew in his throat and penetrated his words. "You are supposed to keep Simone in check."

"She wasn't beside me when I woke," Philippe shrugged. "I found her in the catacombs sitting by Pappy's tomb rambling about singing horses and dancing dogs."

Beneath his mask, Erik's cheeks heated to an uncomfortable level. If there was one place he didn't like his daughter playing, it was in cellars. Keeping his past as The Phantom of the Opera hidden from his children was already a challenge, yet he couldn't blame her for visiting the tomb of that old curmudgeon who had traveled with them year after year. Pappy had been as a grandfather to her.

Simone's cheeks plumped with her smile, softening the edges of his ire. That smile was capable, for now, of drawing the attention away from the stark ridges of visible bone and twisted areas of muscle marring her face. Her tiny voice was tinged with an unusually haunting timbre, its resonance defying her seven years.

"Papa, I have a flower for you." She thrust it forward, her small fist landing squarely in his gut.

Erik suppressed a groan and knelt. He brushed a wayward curl from her forehead and watched her eyes cross as it sprung back into shape. Simone's untamed hair cascaded around her shoulders and tumbled down her face hiding some of it from his view. With her hair lying that way she was as beautiful as any little girl, until she flipped it off her face revealing the cruel hand fate had dealt her. Her hair could hide her missing ear but ultimately did nothing to conceal her misshaped bones or the yellowed, paper-thin flesh stretching across three-quarters of her face. She had his looks, his voice, and the fantastic quality of his

19

eyes. All Erik had to do was shift their position slightly into a shadow, and her eyes would flash an eerie, yet captivating shade of gold. Erik's fingers rippled across her deformity as if doing so would brush away the guilt he carried for creating that part of her. Little girls should look like angels, not bear the curse of a face of Death.

He took her gift, somewhat remorseful over the flower's untimely demise. Perhaps accepting it would lessen the blow of what he was about to tell her. Born without breath in her body until a dedicated doctor saved her life, she thought and reacted differently than most children. "Simone," he gently explained as he rose, "horses cannot sing."

"Yes, they can." The violin thumped against her thigh as she made a Maypole of his legs.

He looked at Anna. She carried plates from the counter to the table and shared a laugh with Brother Lukas. They shrugged in unison, unwilling to touch such a statement. Simone was a mystery, a little enigma that had everyone wrapped neatly around her pinky.

"Horses sing *Alouette*," she insisted. "And dogs dance to it. They did so in the church before the spooky man lit it up with fire."

Plates crashed to the floor in a thunderous explosion circling a target of clay throughout the kitchen. Erik's eyes darted from his daughter's yelp to Anna in time to see her face blanch.

"Philippe, take your sister," he snapped. "Bathe her and get her a clean frock. I need to speak to your mother alone."

"I think not." Philippe's voice felled the room silent. "If Simone saw something—"

"Simone saw nothing," Brother Lukas quietly assured. "Children are to obey their elders, Philippe."

"But we've been trying to uncover what happened to the church for weeks now. How do *you* know she didn't see anything? She clearly *heard* something."

"It's likely her imagination," the monk replied. "Do as your father asks."

Erik was inches away from losing his patience. Philippe could challenge him on any topic under the sun; disobey him on thousands of battlegrounds, but not this one. Not with the gravity of what Simone just said.

"Her imagination?" Philippe pursed his lips and shook his head. "Simone, did you make that up?"

Simone had stopped rounding her father, one hand still on his leg the other clutching the violin to her chest. She ignored the question and instead stared intently at the pattern of clay chips on the floor. "Broken plates tingle my toes."

Philippe rolled his eyes. "Simone?"

Shaking her head, Simone shrugged and looked up. "The horse sang off key. I know because I saw brown."

As Simone rounded her father's leg once more, Anna's hand shot out to her side to steady herself with a nearby chair.

"What Simone heard is obviously linked to my father's colored past, judging from my mother's reaction." Philippe pointed out, folding his arms in a victory stance.

The air burst out of Erik's lungs as he pivoted toward Philippe, breaking Simone's grip on him. Erik hunched into his shock, approaching his son with undisguised curiosity. For years he had made it a point to keep all details of his past away from his children. Though he regretted ever telling the monk of his history, he knew the man of God would never betray him to his kin. Saving the village from illness years ago had been Erik's saving grace and security. There was not a man in the village that wouldn't protect Erik and his family. His son continued to speak with the arrogance of a king causing his eyes to narrow.

"My *colored* past?" He chanced a look at Anna. Her scowl had deepened.

Philippe scoffed. "You don't think I believe we wandered from vagabond camp to vagabond camp across France all those years because it was the life of comfort you so sought for me?"

The corner of Erik's lip twitched as he tried to govern his shock.

"So, you will continue this conversation with me present," Philippe instructed. "It involves the church and Chagny as evidenced by the mention of *Alouette*." He made a casual gesture toward Simone who was staring again, perplexed by the pottery on the floor.

The silence in the room could have made hair stand on end. "Chagny?" Anna gasped incredulously. "What know you of Chagny?"

"I know enough; anytime men with rifles arrived at a camp, we had to run. You and Father switched from German to speaking French. I caught on years ago that there was something you didn't want me to know. Simone may not speak a lick of French, but I taught myself it quite easily. I'm fluent." Philippe spread his hands. "Surprise."

The only movement in the room was Simone as she kicked a wayward shard back into place near the rest of the shattered plates. The scrutiny of Philippe's unblinking eyes bore into Erik, yet he was too shocked to do anything other than listen in a dumbstruck and smoldering silence. The carefully constructed secrets of his past had suddenly cracked open out of the blue, spilling the letters of disaster at his feet.

"One of the armed gents, a bizarre, detached sort of fellow, always hummed *Alouette*." Philippe's causal comment sank Anna into a chair. "I've wondered about your secrets for too long. I understand more than you realize. The Brothers here have been my family, so if I can help solve what happened to the church, I will."

Erik had a pounding headache on the prowl. "Someone remove my daughter from this room immediately. I will not have her innocence manipulated. My son's already is."

"Stop overprotecting her, Father, and cease treating me like an infant. Simone isn't able to comprehend a word we're saying no matter the language we speak. You know how backward her mind is. If you're in trouble, I can help. I spent years without a home, listening to you whisper about Chagny. I'm not stupid. I could see the rifles as clearly as you could. This is my opportunity to know why finally."

"Philippe, I am warning you."

"Warn me all you want. I demand to know."

That was his mother's ever-defiant spirit shining through in him, and he would tolerate it from Anna but not Philippe. Erik didn't think before the tone of his voice switched to one, which was sharp as a bell and hushed as a whisper, able to level the strongest of men into submission. "You demand?"

His freakish voice manipulation yanked Simone's head up from her scrutiny of the floor. She rubbed her ear and swat at the air in front of her. "That wasn't nice. Why did you turn the room red?"

Erik gritted his teeth and prodded her toward Philippe. "Philippe, I am a simple carpenter. Play with your sister."

Philippe was unmoved. He looked at him in such a way Erik couldn't decipher his next move. If he didn't obey so Erik could tend to the shade of white Anna had turned, Erik was going to drag him out of the room by his perfect nose. Instead, Philippe looked from one parent to the other.

"The simple carpenter excuse again, Father? Does that explain why you built a pipe organ in the first place and so painstakingly carved it? Does it explain why locked in a trunk in a secluded room of a monastery there's an opera cloak of the finest quality and a score written in your hand?"

How did he find that trunk? Erik spoke from the side of his mouth. "Are you going to continue this, Philippe?"

"Furthermore there's the matter of that violin Simone carts around." He gestured to the instrument thumping against her thigh as she looked up between the two of them.

Large puffs of breath broke rhythmically through the nose Erik lacked as he walked closer to Anna. He extended a hand to her silently asking her to keep him calm. Erik looked down at her grip on him, surprised at how cold she had gone. He had not played his violin since before Philippe was born. A different time, a different place. Playing, composing, and being one with the magic in his soul had been too risky on the run. It was a silent ghost of his past accidentally found and adopted by Simone.

"No simple carpenter has a violin capable of making the music that one can," Philippe said wondrously. "It has a tone richer than the heavens themselves."

Those words formed a lasso and looped around Erik's neck. They yanked his attention from the grip he had on Anna's hand to his son. "How do you know what that sounds like?"

"I've played it on several occasions."

"*You have what?*" The walls nearly crumbled. His heart pounded in his ears, and he couldn't tell if it was from fury or joy.

"I tried to teach myself with the score in that trunk. But music is damn near impossible to understand. Every note is jumbled upside down and looks backward." He tapped his temple giving his father the first indication of his frustration. "Neither here nor there anyway. Just answer my questions."

Dropping Anna's hand prompted a worried glance from her that Erik ignored. Philippe struck a chord, and it vibrated painfully through every bone in Erik's body. The exchange that happened next flew around the room like a mouse before a cat. There was no place to hide.

"You're not a simple carpenter, Father. With a voice as unique as yours, a score like no other, and the finest of violins? I've heard you and Mother speak of the Opera Garnier."

"That cloak, the violin, they were all in this monastery when we arrived."

"No, they weren't."

"Philippe, I will not tell you again."

"You're a maestro aren't you?"

"Philippe, I am warning you."

"From Paris."

"Philippe—"

"You had an ingénue—"

"I am a carpenter! Now—"

"You're that living myth, that murderer, and maestro, the *Phantom* of the *Opera!*"

FOUR

Unearthly stillness filled the room as if stolen from the depths of the catacombs. Erik paced circles around the central table making the only noise a soft swish of fabric against his legs. For once he was pleased a mask hid his expression.

Sliding his eyes from the monk's sympathetic expression and across the room toward Anna, he noticed her face was so stiff that a feather could have shattered it. Simone had stopped in her tracks, her extraordinary eyes as large as a harvest moon. Philippe's hands had rolled into fists. Erik clamped down on his teeth until his ears rang.

"I will not be hunted!" He would sooner die than be subjected to life as a mongrel on the run again. Striding forward, he stood eye to eye with his son. The black of his mask reflected in the flawless perfection of Philippe's eyes. "Can you handle what you want to know?"

Philippe nodded.

Erik backed away. It mattered not how he knew of The Phantom of the Opera. His legendary past had on more than one occasion been fodder for traveling minstrels. It was all he could do to keep his family out of sight and not dispatch every wandering troubadour he came across. What mattered was how one explains a past of murderous vengeance to a child? How to adequately describe the cancer of madness? The only answer he had was in his daughter's hand.

Simone didn't speak as she looked up at him. His children knew there were times when best not to say a word. Erik walked beyond her rubbing at the headache gnawing at his brain. His son could handle what he needed to know—but could Simone? What *did* she understand, of anything? It was something he never considered. Simone just went through her days with the carefree attitude of butterfly high on nectar. She'd flit from one topic to the next, half the time making little sense to anyone, but melting hearts in the process. How could he upend that? Control over his past, however, had suddenly been yanked from his grasp, leaving him with little choice. Erik rounded, locking eyes with the child staring up at him. She pointed.

"You dropped your flower like *mütter* did the plates."

Erik snatched the violin, ignoring her comment and her heart stabbing cries of outrage that followed. Pacing beyond her, he brushed his thumb across the strings desperate for any sound to drown out her desperation. Simone became his shadow, matching his pace for pace, taking five steps to his every one until Philippe finally grabbed her and held her back. Anyone who disturbed Erik would have done so at his or her own risk as he turned each peg and tuned the long-neglected instrument back into life. He did so silently, every so often meeting the stares upon on him. Simone's was the most intense. Erik turned his back to her, unable to watch her tiny lip quiver, and lifted the violin to his chin. He heard Anna's breath hitch. The bow hovered over the bridge. A bone-rattling battle to command the noise inching into his mind started at his toes and would have vibrated his arm if he didn't fight it back. Noise was his madness...

He wouldn't have it.

The violin became a virgin begging to be stroked, and his soul a man begging to tame her. Feeling his swallow move up and down his throat, Erik touched the bow to the bridge and coaxed the first agonizing notes from the instrument.

Liquid gold tones rose and fell on waves of ecstasy as his feelings transformed from his mind into music—those in the room filled with soundless wonder as he played. Chancing a look at Philippe, Erik's drunken eyes saw his son relax. No longer clenched into his fist, Philippe's elegant fingers took on a life of their own, undulating in tune to the music. There was a repressed maestro in the boy. Erik felt it in his soul. The warmth he felt upon seeing Philippe evaporated to an overwhelming sense of foreboding when he looked at Simone. He knew entirely too well that tiny scowl and the movement of her deep-set eyes as she chased something invisible. Locked within Simone's mind was the same private prison of euphoria only present when Erik composed his most fantastic pieces.

Shaken to the core by that haunting look, he glanced at Anna. She had lowered herself into a chair and was brushing her knuckles slowly back and forth across her lips. She blinked only occasionally, lost in the magnitude of the moment. He knew that look too—the look of the inevitable. Knowing it was too late ever to look backward, Erik nodded to Anna cueing her to tell his story before his resolve crumbled. The pain in his chest broke out upon the strings as music carried her quavering words around the room.

"Philippe, to understand him, is to understand music…"

Time stood still, obeying Erik's every command for change, in the space it took for Anna to explain their history to their children and for him to play out his life. When the last chord rang out, Erik laid the violin and bow on the table. The fingers on his bow arm tingled from overuse. Stretching his hand, he rubbed his upper arm; unconsciously kneading the old gunshot wound that caused his fingers to prickle in the first place. Raoul de Chagny had even marred his abilities with a bow. Looking across the room, the lines of emotion on his son's face were unreadable. The meeting of their eyes caused Philippe to square his shoulders ramrod straight.

"I need air." With that one sentence, Philippe stormed toward the door, threw it open, and disappeared into the morning mist.

Erik should have expected that. The tension in the air was so thick that Brother Lukas' robes could have hung upon it. He paced, rubbing his hand, watching through the open door as Philippe marched in nearly the same manner in the yard. Any concern he had over the tone to Philippe's voice disappeared as a honey-haired devil leaped upon the bench at the table, stopping his heart dead.

"Simone, *nein!*"

Snatching up her beloved instrument and bow, she strangled the violin so tightly in her grip that her knuckles went white. Angry lines marched across her misshapen face, puckering her forehead and making her deformity a ghastly sight to behold. She peered under the violin's bridge before ferociously shaking it.

"How did it make noise?" Bending down, she grabbed the bow and swished it through the air like a musketeer's sword. "Where did it come from? Inside? Do you keep the birds in it, or in my head? How did you get them to color the air?" The violin jabbed up and down in time with her frustration.

Anna crossed the room in a heartbeat, calmly trying to pry the priceless violin from her deathly grip. The girl grabbed the offending instrument to her chest and aimed the bow at her mother's heart.

"The birds flew away! Bring the colors back!" She stomped, rocking the bench as she shook the violin again. "Always too many birds in my head and now they are in *here*? My birds went away, into here, and I want my birds back!"

Erik paused for a second and weighed her words with a leaded-hearted dread. Music and noise often combined in his mind like a cancerous cocktail resulting in years of madness. Never equating it to the likes of birds, he dismissed her comment as the ramblings of a disoriented little girl. Rubbing his temple, he groaned at the battle ensuing between mother and daughter for his beloved instrument. He couldn't look. Nothing survived Simone's curiosity, and lest she snap the priceless instrument in two, he finally cracked. "Let her have it. Just let her have it!"

Simone stomped from the bench to stand squarely on the table. Spoons scattered everywhere. Fist on one hip, the other tucking the violin and bow under her arm like a brilliant concertmaster, she leaned as far forward as she dared and challenged Brother Lukas. "Make him tell me how he did that. Tell him to give me back my birds. They belong in here." She pointed to her head. "He cannot have my birds." Another foot hit the table. "My birds!"

"Simone, why don't you go outside and try to track down those missing birds?" Brother Lukas urged softly, upon catching the warning look Erik sent his way. "Find them and return them to the violin."

The room hung on her next move. Nobody dared to make a peep or move a muscle as the child eyed each one of them. When through, Simone jumped off the table and tramped out the door pointing an accusatory bow at her father.

"The birds are mine."

Dumbfounded silence filled the room as the swirl of curls disappeared out the door.

"All in all that was a mild confrontation between Simone and a new situation, I'd say," Brother Lukas observed. He waited until Anna sank back into her chair before speaking again. "If you two started this, you both had better be prepared to finish it."

"Why?" Erik whispered, shutting the door behind Simone. Maybe it would lock out his past. "I spent a good portion of my life keeping secrets locked away. It makes things tidy."

"You've no choice now. Those children are going to question this, and you better figure out the answers." He looked out the window toward Philippe. "That boy is going to want to know why his maestro of a father has chosen to settle in an area like this, composing arias for monks and for a God in which he has no faith. You can't just tell them you were a reclusive maestro at the Garnier. He will ask specifics about this manhunt, your asylum here, and more about the Phantom. I'll not even ponder what might be going on in the little one's mind." The monk paused. "Does this have anything to do with who Simone saw?"

Sparks rushed down Erik's spine. "I can fix an organ. I can

design a church. I cannot fix the *innocence of my family!*" His shout echoed into the fireplace. Not even Brother Lukas' ever-calm expression was a comfort. Erik walked to the fire and braced himself against the mantel. He clutched the wood, sensing that the heat he felt against his legs was hell cracking open. Pure hatred poured out of his words and into the dancing flames. "Only one man I know sings *Alouette*."

"Loup," Anna whispered. Erik turned to look at her. She caressed a scar upon her temple, panic eddying her words. "We have to tell the children everything. If Chagny and Loup have found us here—then they need to know. Philippe will understand."

"Will he, Anna?" That was a loaded question.

Anna dug at the wood of the table with a finger. Encouraged only by Brother Lukas' nod did she continue. "We answer whatever questions he has. He'll understand."

"And what of Simone?" Crossing his arms and blocking her words, Erik's defensiveness swelled to the surface. He lifted one gnarled finger in the direction of the monk reminding him to mind his tongue. All the Brothers were far too protective of the child, but none more so than one who shared her curse. "You are so confident the boy will understand what went on in that opera house? *Fine*. So he understands. Shall we take it a step further to before you arrived? Perhaps I confirm his suspicions of my great ingénue, sing him some tunes from those operas I taught Christine; fill him in on the chandelier and the concierge I killed; share my affinity for English sweets and a mindless box keeper; lay out the plans for him of my house below ground; and perhaps mentioned a torture chamber or two. Why not a scorpion or a grasshopper? Jolly high! Which will *he* turn? If he likes *that* I can show him more than just my skills on a violin, maybe he would enjoy the silk rope!" Erik's voice swelled as he pushed off the mantle and came toward her.

"Better yet let us go further! *Persia was an absolute delight!*" He punched the air with a fist. "Some of my finest work occurred before the Shah!" Palms to the table, he leaned in, searing Anna with his stare. "I am convinced after that he would be so drunk with happiness he would be dying to know his father spent the better half of his boyhood as the alluring Living Corpse." The fingers on his hand sprung open as he yanked his mask off and thrust it across the room. "How wonderful it will be for him to know I traveled from flea riddled fair to flea riddled fair with my managers singing like a *damned deformed canary!*"

Erik cleared the contents from the top of the table with one violent swing of his arm. Bowls and spoons flew everywhere. Anna pushed to her feet and came to Brother Lukas' side.

"Erik that was unnecessary," she snapped.

"None of this should be necessary!" Erik plucked at the flesh near his temple as if his fingers were beaks pecking into his brain. "You have this belief that everyone will understand and accept as you do. Accepting me is not easy, even for a genius like Philippe and a simple child as Simone. You know what *is* necessary? If we want the children to know, then *I* need to know. After all these years, why, Anna? Why has it been so easy for you to understand me?"

The silence pouring off of her body was an enemy not to be tested. She turned to the monk but said not a word.

Reading her expression, Brother Lukas stood. "I will mind the children."

Brother Lukas was halfway out the door when Erik agreed. "I think you should."

Once alone, he stood like a mountain waiting indignantly for her response. The fire popped; a pistol cueing their fight into motion.

"Brussels," she bit.

"Lovely city, wonderful potatoes."

"I was sixteen before I came to Paris, and staying in Brussels with my father along with Laroque and Wischard."

Erik's eyes pinched, and he dropped his sarcasm. "I thought you did not know the managers of the Opera Garnier before your arrival at my Opera House."

"I lied. They were the great trio of Europe, running cons left and right through every major city they came across. I was the annoying little attachment that came with Barret. My job? Pick pockets mostly. I'm quite good at it." She leaned into him and mocked his previous soliloquy. "Perhaps I can teach it to Simone." Anna walked to the far side of the room, the hem of her skirts swishing angrily. "Pick the pockets when I told, divert police when I told, shag who I was told."

Erik tightened his jaw. He glanced out the window. The thought of her lying with any man roiled his blood.

"You want to know why I understand your life, Erik? Then look at me!"

Trepidation spread through his veins. Slowly looking over his shoulder, his gaze slid up her body until they clasped the fury behind her eyes. He wasn't sure he wanted her to continue.

"They gambled—a lot and usually won. Until the night they met their match in Duke de Molyneux and his son. One particular evening, they lost. They were about to pay the money owed when they had a wonderfully wicked idea. Trade me instead. The Duke's heir was a strapping young man, had everything in his life handed to him on a silver platter. Imagine my shock when I was on that platter. I was upstairs sleeping in a small corner of the floor reserved for the dog and me when the games began. It's a lovely feeling to be gambled away to a spoiled boy for his adolescent need for pleasure. I fought him with everything I could muster until the duke thought it might be fun to join his son."

The usual soft German lilt to Anna's voice turned uncharacteristic, instantly filling him with remorse. It was never his intent to make her so rattled. Erik retrieved his mask and placed it back on. Perhaps it would shield him from her words. "Anna, stop," he pleaded.

"Two men, *at the same time* taking what they wanted, laughing and raping me, while my father stayed downstairs smoking a cigar."

"Stop, now."

"Do you know what I did, Erik?"

"Anna, please. There is no need."

"I was streetwise by that time and smart enough to hide a knife within my reach. The boy was easy. He was my size. But the duke—*took a few tries.*"

32

"Cease!"

"I eventually gave up; he was too strong. But I at least had the chance to run. The duke should have considered himself lucky the chest wall is a difficult thing to puncture for a girl of my size."

"Anna."

His pleas were useless. Anna's words were tumbling over each other in her haste to get them out. Erik could nearly taste their heat.

"I understand because I know what it's like; the sudden surge of power as if you are the Supreme Being able to defend against any who hurt you. Murder can feel good."

The passion in her words shot right up Erik's spine and plunged a knife into his heart. His eyes flew open. She didn't just say that. Erik took two strides toward her, ready to grab her and force that confession back into her soul. "Anna?"

She twisted her way across the room avoiding Erik's attempts at reaching her. "It can feel good until you realize what you've done, and the fear takes over, and you run! I ran as far as I could all the while, my father chasing me through alleyways until a crossroad by a Brussels street. He caught up to me. I still had the knife, and I used it again. But the one man I wanted to kill so badly, I couldn't. So I ran into a crowd and never stopped." Anna had woven her way toward the back door. "Every waking minute I spend wondering how my hands could have killed a boy my age. Praying somehow I could forgive myself. Praying every morning that someday I can look my son in the eyes and not see *that* boy's face. Pondering how to turn back time knowing since the day Philippe was born the same huntsman whose sworn duty it was to find me, is hunting him. I'm *Alouette*, Erik! I'm the lark Loup wants to skin. He's only connected to Chagny because he wants me, and I'm with you!"

"Anna—"

"*Leave me alone!*" She flung Erik's arm aside as he reached for her.

Before he had a chance to utter a further word, the door she yanked open and ran through banged against the wall before bouncing back in its frame leaving the room eerily silent.

Numbed, Erik sank to his hearthside chair. He could feel the gravity of her words make his legs heavier as he sat there. Nothing could have prepared him for that admission. Anna, a murderer? He rested his forehead in his hands, trying to force away the image of Anna committing that horror for a scrap of respect and honor. It was her own form of madness, and she hid it from him for so long. Suddenly, her ability to understand his madness made sense. Why couldn't life remain as it was mere hours ago—basic in contrast to their pasts? His fingers pulsed against his temples like a spider sucking on a meal. An unwelcome thought crept into his mind and spread like that spider's web. What was life like at Chagny? What life had Raoul built being the hunter and not the hunted?

A log hissed then popped. Erik rolled his head toward it. He finally had embraced the normalcy of the life Philippe de Chagny wanted for him—but at what cost? Meddling man! Regret seeped into Erik's soul. He shouldn't think such things. He deeply missed his music and knew he owed far too much of what he had to his old friend. The time had come to merge the past with the present, yet how does one conduct such an opera alone?

Erik stood. Damn if he knew the correct answer. The only thing he did now for sure was Anna needed him. He slipped out the door and found her in the kitchen courtyard. She bobbed up and down as she bent to the ground, muttering nonsensically to herself. The barely budded herbs took her abuse as she snapped off leaves and slammed near dead branches of thyme into an awaiting basket near her feet. Approaching from behind, Erik reached over and put a hand on the back of her neck.

"*Mon Die*—!"

Her fist landed like a shot against his jaw as soon as she rounded, knocking his surprised cry clear off his lips. Erik barely had a chance to blink before years of torment drove forward an uncontrolled fury. Anna scratched and punched, making violent contact with whatever part of him she could.

"Anna!" he shouted. Erik reached at her flailing arms, trying not to harm her as she thrashed. Grabbing her tight to his body, he hauled her kicking and screaming, until his back bumped against the cottage wall. "Anna, hush—Anna! Anna!" Erik lowered them to the ground, cooing softly in her ear as she writhed in his arms like a child trapped before her lifelong monster. "Anna, shhh…"

Cradling her close to his chest, he held her tight against his own racing heart in total understanding of her long overdue release. Erik's heart could have bled through his shirt as Anna broke down sobbing and trembling like a frightened bird. His long, thin fingers entwined with hers.

"These hands did what they had to do." He turned her small hands over in his. "Mine did what I wanted. There is a difference."

Anna pressed her head back against his chest. "I want a normal life! I want my children to understand our pasts, but in the same beat of my heart, I don't want them to know. They're only *children*. I never was a child, Erik. I don't want to ruin their innocence."

"I had no childhood either." He rested his mask against her hair feeling every painful breath she took as she calmed down. "I am living through them, and believe me I do not want it to end. But at some point, they have to know."

"What if that was Loup? What if Simone did hear him? What if we have to leave again? What if the children don't understand?"

There were so many questions their life had created with so few answers, and her questions a part of a test he couldn't master. "If and when the time comes we will deal with it together, and we will tell them, slowly." Reaching around her, he dried her tears. "Thank you, Anna."

She shifted in his lap to look up at him. "For what? Lying for years? Beating you?"

He smiled. She did have a good left hook. "For having me tell them that I am a maestro." His voice filled with enormous passion. "Anna, I have had so much music locked inside of me since we settled here, I feel I can share that now."

He shifted her in his lap and stroked her hair before tasting her tears. One kiss to each eye dipped them closed and drove home his love for her. Music rose in his mind, undulating up and down repeating each note with the beat of his heart. He trailed his lips down her cheek to her nose, all along softly telling her to relax. The music leveled out before skipping through his mind, building and rising with each taste of her. Erik kept their lips as one as he stood, taking her with him. The music that flooded his mind every time he loved her grew louder and louder until it was unbearable, unspeakable.

His eyes snapped open. He tore his lips from hers. Shock held him firmly in place. Around them, falling from the air itself was music unlike any ever heard. He studied Anna's darting eyes.

"Do you hear that?" she said.

"That is not in my mind," Erik replied. "Where is it coming from?"

"I've no idea."

He traced the air with his eyes following the unseen stanzas of music. It guided them around the building to behold a supernatural sight. Erik and Anna stood as still as statues, mimicking the posture of Philippe and Brother Lukas as Simone twirled like a dervish in the courtyard.

Violin against her chin and bow to the strings, she was one with the instrument and the music dancing on the air. The child skipped and spun, painting a story around her with each twirl she made. Erik never experienced anything like it. The music shifted and moved as fast as wildfire. It exploded as passionate as love itself. Dancing and bowing at the same time with her golden curls fanning around her, Simone didn't miss a single note. How she knew to put the notes together, Erik had no idea. The look on her face was a combination of raw madness and utter bliss. He swallowed—hard. He barely heard Anna's stammered question.

"Did you ever? When you were young? How is she…?"

"I do not know. I never did—that."

Transfixed, a foreboding rose in him he dared not express. This—was unnatural. He jolted as the music jerked in a different direction, Simone's chime-like laughter adding to the notes. Her body was an extension of music as she moved. Fear rose up like a ten-horned beast and punched Erik backward. Music, when uncontrolled in his mind, lead to noise and noise drove to madness.

God's blood, his little girl was condemned.

"No!" Panic charged him forward with such ferocity Simone abruptly stopped playing. "Simone, give me the violin."

"*Nein!*" she cried with a fervor he had never heard. "These are my birds. I put them in here now. Leave them alone!"

"Simone, return my violin this instant!"

She bolted out of reach each time he swung for her. Simone dodged between Philippe and Brother Lukas, rounded Anna, ducked around trees… Dumbstruck, the rest of his family was unable to help. Only Erik had the fierce determination to silence what he suspected was on the rise in his little girl. Finally snagging her by one arm, he hauled her firmly to his chest. She writhed like a trapped reptile as she screamed and kicked. Biting his forearm, Simone dropped to the ground taking the beloved instrument with her.

"They are *my* violin birds," she yelled, running out of the yard as fast as her legs could carry her. "You can't have them back."

Erik was about to make chase when Anna clamped his arm. "Let her go. She'll retreat to one of her favorite spots, calm down, and all will be well. This is Simone after all."

Chest heaving, his mind racing with the poison of noise long suppressed, he turned to regard his family and Brother Lukas. His forearm throbbed with the aftermath of a child's wrath.

"That was not Simone," he panted. "That was a petite Phantom."

FIVE

Clouds dimmed the morning sun, draping Paris in a mood-sucking monochromatic gray—although André couldn't be sure that the weather was the culprit. It was either the clouds making him sad or the events of last night. It certainly wasn't leftover champagne fogging his head.

André cinched the belt on his overcoat tighter around his waist and turned the collar up to his neck. He ran a hand through his mist-dampened hair and wandered up and down the rows of plants in *hôtel* Chagny's small courtyard garden carefully selecting the flowers to enhance his bouquet. The flowers should have done their job to brighten his mood; he had an affinity for horticulture after all. It all felt as drab around him as the sky looked.

"Picking flowers. Such a masculine pastime."

André's bouquet fell to his side along with his arm. He looked around the courtyard, his jaw tightening so much he felt it in his ears. He spotted the bounty hunter leaning casually against the central stone memorial.

"You really are as soft as your father," Loup continued. "You should travel with me. I'll teach you what it is like to become truly hard."

"What are you doing here?" Last night's tension wound in André anew. He'd not enjoyed his birthday since Loup showed up.

"Here, as in the garden, or here in general?" Loup indicated a prized rose bush and his English foxhound sniffing about it. "Here I'm allowing my dog to piss. In general, I'm about to head out to find your Phantom."

Arrogant son-of-a-bitch. André jerked his chin in the air. "You haven't found him in sixteen years. You're an incompetent ass."

"Rich, perhaps, but not an ass. I'm merely doing my job."

"That job, Monsieur, does not include engaging my son."

André stifled a huff. Just like his father to show up now, after dismissing André all last night after Loup showed up. He and the hunter turned in tandem as his father approached down the center stone path.

"It's a dreary day for a stroll in the garden, Vicomte," he remarked, making way up the steps to a higher level of the terraced courtyard.

"I was collecting a bouquet for *Maman*. She seemed upset this morning." He studied Loup hoping his father caught his gist. "A pity after a grand celebration."

"The only thing that will ever cheer that woman is a monster in a mask," Loup quirked his brow and yanked on his fob. He spoke to the morning hour. "Don't tell me, Monsieur le Comte. Your Persian fellow denied knowing a thing about the Phantom, but you wish me to be on my merry way nonetheless."

André looked between the two significant figures in his life, his father and the creature that often roamed his nightmares. He waited on an explanation, but his father remained silent. Somehow he wasn't surprised. It seemed like everyone went mum when the bounty hunter arrived. Loup's presence in his life had long been enough to make André want to snap. He represented a menace as much as he did a fascinating, unattainable a part of Chagny's history.

Maybe it was the long night or the weather, or perhaps the realization that for the first time he wanted to be anywhere but Paris that made André scoff. Bugger to all this. He'd had enough of it. "What's going on, *Père*? Loup disappears for an entire year, returns, and you dismiss him overnight? You think I don't notice how unusual that is? The Phantom is near, isn't he? He's been found. If such is the case, then I want to know. I'm the Vicomte de Chagny, and I'll not have that man anywhere near my mother."

"And I'm the Comte de Chagny and head of this family. I don't bow to my son's demands."

The clip to his father's voice took André's bravado and yanked it down to his boots. Right. He was Comte and André was crammed back into that you'll-know-everything-when-you're-old-enough box of his father's. André bit his tongue. He had schoolmates owning their estates by now. Not that he wished any ill on his father; it was just that his frustration was popping in his veins.

"I wish Uncle Philippe were here," he muttered before he had a chance to check his tongue.

André watched those words punched his father harder than a fist of a man five times his size. He turned his back to both of them, refusing to take his words with him. If he had the guts, he would have shoved Loup aside, and off the memorial, he leaned against. Though far from the elaborate crypt at Chagny, the memorial to Philippe commanded an awesome respect and Loup's boots upon its pristine surface sickened him.

"That was an abrupt confession, son. Why does my brother's death concern you now? It never has in the past."

André turned. The mention of his uncle would prompt his father to open up but never the giant well-dressed leech standing next to them. "How would you know *what* concerns me of the past? You never *ask* me. Loup disappeared for a full year only to return and cause you and Jules to whisper and make mother look as though she has seen a ghost. You get that look every time I mention Uncle Philippe, yet hell if anyone talks about him. That's what concerns me."

Loup pushed off the memorial and swung around to snap a branch from a nearby tree. Dewy leaves shook down around them. Leaping like a deranged frog, the bounty hunter drew a

line in the gravel path between father and son.
"Who will cross it first?" he dared, laughing. "I adore a good
row between father and son. No one? I'll go first. Tell me,
Monsieur le Vicomte, what do you understand about those
whispers?" Loup leaned in close to André's ear. "Who killed
your dear old uncle? The same masked man who wants to shag
your mother, and vice versa, or someone else?"

"What?" André's icy gasp colored the morning air around
him a ghostly white. The glare he sent his father could have
pierced him to the garden wall.

"Be on your way!" his father commanded. "We have our
answers from the Persian. Now get underway and don't return
until you have what I want from you."

"What answers?" André pushed away from Loup's absinthe-
coated breath. He hated the smell of licorice. "Did the Phantom
kill Uncle Philippe?" His regarded the wild glee painted on
Loup's face and the rising tension coiling around his father. "I
knew it. I always suspected something happened between the
Phantom and Uncle Philippe. I'm Chagny's heir, *Père*. Back
home I see you sit in silence before his tomb and I've no answers
as to why."

"His tomb and hers," Loup returned to his previous perch and
caressed the two names engraved on the memorial.

André pivoted, his voice as sure as bullets. "If you *ever* speak
of my sister again I'll personally run you through!" Loup lifted
his hand from the memorial and shook them off as if he didn't
like the feel of it on his fingers. André turned to his father, more
and more questions rolling in his mind. He nodded to her name.
"I was told that stress the Phantom placed on *Maman* robbed me
of Evangeline and caused her stillbirth. Now that stress makes
all the more sense."

André finally struck a chord. Several seconds ticked by until
his father's unusually calm voice broke the tension. When his
father was this serious, the outcome was never good. His father
indicated the half done bouquet.

"Your mother will be charmed. Bring them to her and tell her
we're going for a ride. She need not know the reasons. I'll tell

you what I see fit, and you're not to question me further."

André removed a single lily and shoved the balance of the bouquet into his father's chest.

"You give them to her. I may be getting the answers I finally deserved, but it does little to calm the anxiety of years of not knowing." Before he left, he turned to the memorial and laid the bloom beneath. "That one was for Evangeline."

His boots crunched angrily on the pebbled path, the sound beating like a drummer to the answers he was finally to receive. Halfway down the path, he stopped upon hearing Loup shout after him.

"You're welcome. Nothing like a good row, right?"

André looked over his shoulder and saw his father's eyes narrow on the hunter.

"Leave. When you return, you had best show me an end to this nightmare, for second to the Phantom; there is no one I want out of our lives more than you."

That made two of them. The bounty hunter's trademark laugh peppered the air followed by his jaunty rendition of *Alouette*. André hated that song. Loup and the dog nipping at his feet were waltzing away in the opposite direction. It took all André had to look back at his father. When he did, the mountain of tension building on his shoulders crumbled. He watched, remorsefully, as his father pulled a perfect red rose from the bouquet and lifted it to his nose. The rest he lay down at the base of the memorial. André's heart seized to see him press his palm over the name of Philippe Georges Marie. His father's head bowed in a palatable pain that André felt, but didn't understand.

Maybe he would soon.

Mist of a different kind threatened André's eye as he wished his uncle were alive. He watched his father trace Philippe's name until he couldn't take it anymore. André rushed inside.

He could wish all he wanted; nothing could bring back the dead.

→》•·——— ·•·———···《←

The weather wasn't helping matters at the moment. Christine woke in a somber mood, which worsened once she glanced outside and saw the dismal day. She should just dash any hopes she had of her humor improving, especially now since her conversation was getting nowhere. The damp air intensified every scent in the stable making her already sour stomach churn. She'd been up most the night fighting down nausea that had seized her since Loup returned and talking to Raoul wasn't helping it any. Every day since the start of this manhunt sixteen-years ago she had some ailment be it a headache or a belly full of knots. That's the price of guilt and fear she supposed. Christine had learned how to manage it and make the most out of her days, yet right now she wished she were anywhere but in the stables. She endured Raoul's penchant for collecting prized stallions, though she preferred when he doted on his orchids. At least they didn't smell of hay and leather. Couldn't they have this conversation in one of their salons?

Hay swirled around her skirts as she paced. André's celebration seemed a distant memory in light of Loup's surprise arrival. Usually, after such celebration, they'd be still entertaining a straggling guest or relaxing together over tea and a good book. A stroll among the stalls had replaced that. Ordinarily being around the horses relaxed her husband, but judging by the way his jaw tightened making his mustache lift, he was anything but focused. Perhaps he missed his vast holdings at Chagny, and it was time to return from their Paris holiday. Or maybe his aggravation stemmed because of the ice she had doused on what had been a bonding afternoon with his son. Christine could practically see pools of water gathering at Raoul's feet. Legard walked next to him, crop taping lightly against his gloved palm. The subtle tick, tick, tick it made was beginning to get on her nerves. Christine gave up her pacing and stayed in place, her invisible pitcher of ice water in hand.

"I merely feel as his mother I'm in within my right to know what you told him. You took Legard along for a morning ride to tell our family history to our son and left me behind? Not to mention you never sought my approval of it in the first place."

Raoul's mustache twitched again, a sure-fire sign his temper was rising. He did an excellent job of hiding it in horseflesh.

"I don't need my wife's approval for anything." He spoke toward the stallion he stroked "What do you wish of me? André had questions about Loup's arrival, and I gave him answers."

"He had questions *only* about his arrival?" There was more to this, she could feel it, and Christine didn't like her husband's blunt reply. Raoul could be harder than marble to crack sometimes, so she looked to Legard for answers.

As if picking up on the cue—or replying for her husband so that he didn't have to—Legard spoke. "We discussed Philippe in addition to my visit with the Persian."

Christine felt the hairs stand up on the back of her neck. Going to visit that Persian fellow to seek answers about Erik was a warning shot louder than a canon. This manhunt was about to spiral out of control again. Raoul continued to reach into a stall to comfort a neighing horse, flaring Christine's desire to rip his hand out and slap him senseless with it. He and Legard were up to something. Petting a horse would do nothing help calm the rising storm.

"He's old enough to know," Raoul declared. "That includes knowing that we're inches away from finding the Phantom. What is your misgiving over this?"

"What makes you say I've any misgivings?" She had plenty of them, not that she was about to let on and have them ruin her life.

"For one, your unusual silence since Loup arrived. Second, you disrespect my role as head of this family and how I elect to raise my heir." His forearm rested on a stall door as he continued to click off his list. "Third, when the pitch of your voice rises you're either hiding something or as nervous as a newly trained diva."

"Hiding something?" Christine poked a strand of hair behind her ear, even though she knew it to be perfectly pinned down. "Don't be ridiculous."

"See. There's that pitch again. It's time this family was involved in this manhunt at the same level. Answers as to my brother's death depend on it."

She slapped her hand down to her side. "Erik had nothing to

do with Philippe's death. That theory obsesses you. Don't allow it to color our son's perceptions."

"Don't allow it?" Raoul jolted backward. "I'll not allow it, so long as your obsession is removed from the palette as well."

A rock developed in her throat. She feared the lump was visible. "What are you talking about?"

"Erik."

That name was a hot iron right to her heart.

"If we tell André everything that went on in the Opera Garnier," Raoul continued, his stern look added to her ill ease, "all about your 'Angel of Music' and the Phantom of the Opera, then why not tell André about your obsession with *Erik* also."

"I have no obsession with Erik, be him Angel, Phantom or just a man. You're the one hunting him down."

Lies rolled off her tongue like spun silk. Christine had become expert at weaving them when it came to Erik. She'd think of him daily whether a wandering thought or a deliberate cry for him in her soul. But if she was obsessed with anyone it was Anna Barret. Christine tried *not* to think of her. That woman was a poison that polluted the air she breathed. Throughout the years Christine figured the more she convinced herself of that, the easier it would be to push away the truth about this manhunt. Erik had saved her life from a horrible man, yet her fostered jealousy toward Anna had created an avalanche of untruths.

Reaching into a stall, she took a cue from her husband and rubbed the soft muzzle of a mare. It did nothing calm her unease. She perpetuated this manhunt and her conscious knew it. Lying to her husband went against how she was raised, and every mass she sat through felt like sitting on a bed of hot coals. The lies, the guilt, the manhunt itself could have been over years ago if she told Raoul that Erik had saved her life. But would Raoul have ever believed her? Vengeance still would have seen Erik put to death. And then there was the matter of her heart. Avalanches, as she learned, tended to smother those buried beneath them.

"I hunt him for you," Raoul snapped back. "For a promise I made to you and one I made to myself that Philippe's death wouldn't be ignored."

"You're the only one who believes Erik had anything to do with Philippe's drowning on the shores of that lake beneath the opera."

"That's unfair, Christine," Legard tried to interject.

She turned to him. "Is it? Look me in the eye and show me then, *Inspector Legard*, that you have any proof. If you did, would you be scampering off to bother an old Persian every time we met with a dead end? You're André's godfather. Step in and protect him. You've become a hunter worse than Loup."

"So have you," Raoul pointed out. "Do you think I don't know your reasons for reacting with such bliss every time we meet with dead ends?"

"Bliss? You know I want nothing to do with Erik. I want him captured as much as you do. I merely regret the years this has stolen from my family."

Christine started pacing again, studying the dust around her boots instead of Raoul's disgust.

"Your life has been one of comfort through this all, Christine. Nothing has been stolen from us except time. And you want *everything* to do with that man. I meet dead ends, and your spirits lift. You think I don't see it, but I do. We come inches from news of Anna Barret, and suddenly you're a fox on the chase. We come to perhaps finding both of them—and you fall silent." He nodded, indicating the small skip in her step. "Even now it betrays you. Your jealousy of that woman is inconceivable. It's not enough that I've given you everything I possibly can and went to hell and beyond for you. No, it's not enough for *me* to love you, you need him as well."

"Raoul," Legard softly called.

Christine yanked her head up so suddenly it spun for a second. She lifted a hand in the air; her palm open between her and Legard. Though she appreciated his attempt to calm the rising tone in her husband's voice, she privately admitted to needing to know his suspicions.

Raoul waved their friend aside. "I want to find him so he can pay his debt to society for the murders he's committed, for the injustice against Chagny and to pay for the torment he put you through. Do you think that I'm so naive after all these years not to realize when I share my bed with you, in your mind's eye you love him?"

Christine's hand lowered like a bird plummeting from the sky with breast of lead shot. She stared, unseeing at the hay beneath her feet. Although that confrontation brewed for years, she never expected it to make her feel so dazed. When she looked up again, Raoul's back was turned to her as he stared intently down the stable toward the courtyard beyond. Glancing to Legard, she noted his folded arms and downtrodden stare.

"My fidelity is yours, Raoul. I gave you my life and our children."

She saw him stiffen. There was no way she could tell Raoul the feelings she had told Erik in the opera house so long ago. That she loved her husband with all her heart, but Erik with all her soul. Was loving from the heart or the soul more powerful? How could anyone save her understand what it was like to be chosen by the Angel of Music? What it meant to love two men ardently, but differently.

She turned to a nearby mare and stared into her brown eyes. She barely saw her reflection in them and prayed the truth would remain hidden behind them. When she began thinking of Erik, it was hard to hide the gleam in her eyes. Lord, yes, she loved Erik. She longed to experience the man his kiss once showed him to be, not an Angel, not a Phantom, but her dark, mysterious, and deeply sensual man. Christine inched her head over her shoulder to look at Raoul. She needed them both, didn't she? Raoul was her necessity in life, the Phantom her pure desire. Lord, how to separate the two? She didn't want to. She loved them both.

"I gave you our children," she whispered, begging her soul not to betray her true feelings. "You've nothing to say to that?"

Raoul glanced beyond the courtyard to the direction of Chagny. She caught his eye when he moved. The mention of their children, not just André, lifted sadness behind his eyes. Losing their baby due to the stress of a manhunt was just one more lie she tattooed upon her soul.

Closing her eyes, she fought aside the memory of Loup

shoving her while pregnant down that flight of stairs. If only she had consented to his blackmail demands immediately. Evangeline died because of Loup's abuse and his threats upon Christine's life. She was desperate to spare Raoul the scandal her secrets would bring Chagny. Even in that death, Raoul blamed Erik. In it all Christine blamed herself, but there was no way to climb free of her lies. She loved Erik, she had always loved him, and if she had to choose right at this moment, she would choose...

André.

Oh dear God.

Her son! Christine pressed a shaking hand to her mouth. What was she doing? Selfishly trying to decide which man would love her more, her husband or the Phantom, when the one who loved her the most was barely a man.

Christine felt her cheeks drain of color. Coming up behind her husband, she wrapped her arms around his waist. "I chose you, Raoul. From the beginning, I chose you, and now you and André." She nodded at Legard silently asking for his help as well. "Deal with the Persian, tell our son what you will, do what you may with Loup. Find Erik."

The words may have popped out her mouth, but they weren't the truth of her heart.

Don't find, Erik! I pray you will never will, so help me; I pray you never will!

She reached up and brushed her lips softly to her husband's. She secretly forced her soul to obey her, lying to the voices in her mind to do battle with her demons; the longing she so desperately had for a man she should not love.

Six

Anna compared the sun and the shadow of a tree. She had been waiting for nearly thirty minutes. With no roof overhead, the late afternoon sun beat upon her shoulders and made the granite flecks in the stones around her glimmer to life. Squinting did little to lessen the glare. What had been the church stood in throbbing silence despite the chattering birds. She watched as Erik moved among the rubble knowing it was best to be patient. He was an ardent disbeliever in God. He didn't come here to mourn what the building represented. With his face perpetually caged, Anna had come to learn the small twitches of his hands or slight tilts to his head that betrayed his moods. This time around Erik was taking unusually long to survey the damage he had already scrutinized to the nth degree. When he came to the steps that had once led to the organ every move he made, slowed. Erik was in a foul mood.

"You're contemplating telling him everything, aren't you, beyond your history as a reclusive maestro. That's why you're roaming among the rubble."

Anna wasn't surprised when Erik didn't reply. The subject had been capped weeks ago, leaving her to deal with the fissure created between father and son. He and Philippe were often at odds. They were two genius minds continually working to trump one another. Since learning his father was a maestro, something had shifted in Philippe. The boy long adored music. Ever since he was young, Philippe would soak up all he could at village fairs and often spent time with the monks as they played Erik's organ. There was heaviness on her heart as she watched Erik kick at the charred wood where the magnificent instrument once stood. In the pile of blackened timber were soot-darkened pipes, and a broken manual grinned upward like rows of decaying teeth. Erik had refused to touch the instrument after he built it, even refused to speak about music, a point Philippe never understood until now. With the new revelations regarding Chagny and the manhunt, it became all too obvious just how sharp Philippe's mind truly was, leaving Anna to ponder how much longer her son wouldn't press the issue.

Erik turned to stare down the center aisle to where she stood. Anna patiently folded her hands over the basket of eggs she held for the market. She knew he wouldn't answer her query. Standing there, in fading sunshine, dressed head to toe in black with his face still, unnecessarily, concealed behind a mask, a foreboding god-like quality poured out his stance. It sent a ripple down her spine. She had thrilling respect for Erik's power and passion, and melancholy realization of how he came to be that way. He was a living oxymoron. Fitting into this sort of world—but not. She lifted her chin higher in surprise when he spoke.

"Philippe, I could use your help with what is left of the organ," he called.

Anna glanced over her shoulder toward where Erik looked. Philippe stood at what had been the door, refusing to enter the charred remains of the building. In the street beyond, the village vibrated with its usual pace. Carriages rumbled down the road and townsfolk hustled about. The realization of his father's odd history at the Garnier was a mantel on his young shoulders more so then the sack of wool slung over them. Philippe didn't move beyond shifting his weight to his opposite leg. Impatient as always. Some things never changed. Anna repressed a need to sigh and glanced from son to father.

"Does that reply answer your question, Anna?" Erik frowned. Anna opened her mouth to reply but shut it at the sound of a twittering violin. She had to grin. There may be a riff between Philippe and Erik, but Simone was positively vibrant. The violin had not ceased its music since she found a way to bring out those silly birds in her head. Her current tune mirrored her nimble mischief—warbling notes up and down like the call of a far-off blackbird. Anna's grin grew as she saw Philippe roll his eyes skyward. Impatient though her son may be he had a special tolerance for Simone. She walked in circles near her brother as she played, never once paying any regard to the chatter of villagers as they paused to listen before continuing on their way. Though she had a mysterious gift for music, it came at a concerning price that Anna tried not to think about. Simone preferred the music of late, allowing notes to fall out of her fingers instead of words out her mouth.

Burying that worry in the recesses of her mind, Anna flicked her gaze from Simone and back to Erik. He had not relaxed since Simone found her music, and seeing her march around Philippe only stiffened him more. It did nothing of the sort for Anna. Despite her lack of speech, the ease in which Simone played was an enigmatic blessing. In light of the idea that Chagny had been lurking in the area weeks ago, coupled with Philippe's brooding war with his father, Anna looked to find anything that was a simple joy. To Erik, it seemed Simone's music was a potential curse upon them all.

"Simone!"

Philippe's cry snapped Anna out of her introspection and her heart slamming against her ribs. She spun toward him at the sound of his call, sending eggs flying out of the basket and splattering at her feet. Erik raced passed her in a blur of black. Anna followed as fast as her legs could carry her.

"She was playing and out of nowhere—a rock!" Philippe's breath was clipped and his neck a rising shade of red.

Simone had collapsed, cowering at her brother's feet. Wide-eyed and dazed with one tiny hand coated with the blood still trickling from her temple, she stared at the red-tinted stone at her feet. Philippe's head volleyed around him as his chest began to heave. Anna swore his expression would melt iron.

"Simone?" Erik softly called sinking to his knees.

Simone blinked as if trying to make sense of something senseless. She stopped staring at the rock and looked at her father with a heart-stopping expression. "Somebody knocked my birds quiet and made the notes blue. They're scary."

Anna knew that look. She had seen it hundreds of times before in her life, always when a situation arose that Simone didn't understand. She had no explanation for Simone's odd choice of words, but they didn't bother her. Simone had always twisted common things together in a way that would make sense to none but her. Erik's expression Anna didn't need to see and definitely didn't need to question. A pole seemed to replace his spine.

"I'm sure a carriage kicked up a rock," she reassured. She reached out to undo the kerchief at her daughter's neck. Simone stared at her, although her eyes seemed unseeing. "All will be well, *mäuschen*."

"No one is going to hurt her and get away with it." Philippe's hands had balled into fists as he searched around him. He started toward a crowd at the green, but Erik's hand shot out. It encircled his wrist.

"Philippe, no."

"No? People can't just—"

"People are a despicable lot. They can and they will."

Erik's tone was gentle enough so not to frighten Simone any more but its undercurrent coursed with repressed outrage.

"I'm confident it was just a carriage," Anna insisted as Erik continued to study her wound. A seven-year-olds world is only so big, and the thought of prejudice shrinking her daughter's world was a fear for her that Anna had been battling since her birth. They refused to see her masked merely to spare man their misgivings about those who looked different.

"How can you be so cavalier?" Philippe was incredulous. "People can granted, but they won't because I'll not have it!"

Anna held her hand up insisting her son remain calm. She

patted his arm, acknowledging the dismay that made him shuffle. "Philippe, enough."

Simone picked up the rock and rolled it around in her hands, her long hair scattering around her lap like a security blanket.

"No," Philippe replied, trying to play one parent against the next. "Look at her, Father. Simone doesn't understand these things. We can't just let this go."

Anna bit her tongue. A battle was not exactly appropriate right now. Philippe was Simone's exclusive champion, and at times like this, his passion to protect could be all-consuming.

Erik carefully lifted bloody hair out of the wound strand by matted strand. "Simone understands in ways she knows how. I always did."

"It was a carriage." Anna balled the kerchief in her hand. Making a fist around something secretly felt good. Placing a kiss on her daughter's head, she nodded toward distant creek snaking the outskirts of the village center. "I'll soak this in water, and we can wash this all away. A carriage is to blame, nothing more."

Heading off, she rubbed her temple. Looking behind her to where Simone sat, Erik doting on her and Philippe standing sentry, only made the tension coiling around her head worse. Even from a distance, she could tell that Simone's hurt went far deeper than a cut on her head.

I wish I could crawl into that child's mind and understand how she puzzles through things like this. Anna sighed to herself. The music Simone would play after this would shift, perhaps a long and sad piece. The tunes seemed to match her expression, and all Anna saw now behind the fear in her haunting eyes was the same distant regard for the world present in Erik's.

Coming upon the brook, she knelt at the water's edge and soaked the kerchief. The sunlight shimmered off the water. As much as she wanted to believe it, it wasn't a carriage. Their sleepy village teemed with hunters gearing up for stag season. It was only a matter of time before Simone had a taste of the world that lay beyond the village. A taste of how some people would embrace her with compassion while others would shun her in fear. Anna twisted the kerchief wringing out her frustrations into the brook. *Come what may I won't see her masked.*

Glancing over her shoulder toward the green, Anna watched as Simone curled her hand over her face and placed the red stone in her pocket. The memory of this would be a scar her daughter would keep forever. And Erik? Anna could see the agony pouring off of him over Simone's confusion and pain.

She twisted the kerchief harder as her heart shattered a thousand times for her child, making the water distort the quivering reflections of the trees overhead. As the water rippled outward toward the bank, a warped faced appeared peeking through the leaves. Anna cocked her head and leaned down to study the reflection.

What on earth?

A gasp burst out of her mouth seconds before her chest seized. Her blood ran frigid, too cold to even bother to flow. Anna could barely lift her eyes from the reflection to the wet boots of the man looming over her.

"*Mon Alouette.* It's been awhile hasn't it?"

Water smacked her in the face as the man slammed a fistful of rocks into the creek. Bile shot to her throat. She barely was able to scratch out his name. "Loup."

"Oh, *mon Aloutte*, say it again."

A lewd moan snaked out his mouth seconds before he lunged. The hand he clamped over her mouth crammed Anna's scream down her throat. Panic blinded her while tree branches lashed her skin and tore at her ankles as she was dragged away. She felt the air in her lungs bang against her chest as Loup shoved her against a tree trunk.

"I knew you were here when I burned down that church. Why do you look so shocked to see me?" Loup's teeth slammed against hers as he ravaged her mouth with his unforgiving greeting. He broke the kiss to whisper hotly in her ear. "Your old friend the comte wants proof that you and your lover are here. He'll get more than proof, won't he?" Loup nodded back toward the green. "I suspect your Phantom will be hard with anger when he finds you missing. He'll come running after you doing my job for me making a dull manhunt a pure delight! I get to sit back and enjoy the show. Life is beautiful!"

Anna's heart threatened to pound out her chest as Loup hauled toward a clearing. Branches and bushes broke as he forced her through the under canopy. She fought, but he held her so tightly it was all she could do to breathe. As soon as he gave her some slack so to undo the tether on his horse, she thought to run, but the hounds began crawling from out of the underbrush. They came one by one, from every direction, from every bush, heads down and hackles up.

If she had one phobia, it was dogs.

"Tell me *mon Aloutte*, did you miss me?" Loup snatched her by the waist and hauled her in close. Tears sprung to her eyes. Anna bit her cheek until she tasted blood refusing to look at him. Everywhere else she could see salivating dogs. Loup nipped a path up her neck stilling her ability to scream.

"You've been busy," he cooed "You've children. Your daughter is positively horrific. I hope that rock didn't hurt her. I couldn't resist a bit of target practice." He circled the inside of her ear with this tongue forcing her to swallow down her already digested breakfast. "Why so quiet, *Alouette*? I tell you, this hunt has kept me engaged over all these years, but nothing is quite so sweet as holding your trophy buck. Surely you knew the comte employed my services? He'll be pleased, as will others who are dying to see you." He stressed his words, his smile leaching a perverse satisfaction. "Mainly a certain Belgian duke."

"I don't know what you're talking about," she whispered shakily.

"I figured you'd say that. But no fears, you'll soon find out."

The crushing force of his lips against hers stifled Anna's cry, squeezing moisture out her eyes. Thrashing her head side to side, she shook him off.

"So sweet a reunion," Loup laughed.

Her world pitched sideways as he swung her up onto the horse. Dogs leapt and snapped at her feet. Body rigid with fear, she was powerless to stop the inevitable as Loup mounted behind her and spurred the horse into action.

Erik's name tore from her soul seconds before the horse

bolted forward leaving the village clueless to her absence.

On the opposite end of the treeline, away from the babbling brook, life went on as usual in the village. Simone's eyes were closed. She perched on the railing of a fence near the village center, her head moving gracefully back and forth in time with the sad, yet perplexing tune weeping out her violin. Erik folded his arms across his chest as he waited on Anna's return with the wet kerchief and attempted not to stare at the bright red mark upon Simone's temple. Philippe leaned against the fence, studying each villager that past as if they were all suspect. Several folks they knew stopped to listen and comment over Simone's unheard of new gift. Erik treated them with more benefit of the doubt than his son did. Hearing his name, he turned as the portly owner of the post wobbled in his direction. The man paused to listen to the mournful notes for a moment before handing Erik a letter and hastening off.

Beneath his mask, Erik's face skewed as much as Simone's music shifted. Livelier notes skipped on their air as she hopped off the fence to play merrily to the flock of chickens pecking their way across the green. Nothing seemed to impact her for long. Whatever her thoughts, they'd shifted away from the cut on her head and lifted Erik's heart from his stomach back to its rightful place. His nerves, however, stood at the ready.

Once sure Simone was contented being a Pied Piper to a bunch of hens, he glanced at the note with circumspect caution. Odd. It was addressed to him care of the abbot. Wrinkled and stained, it had undergone quite a journey to find him. Erik unfolded the letter.

> *If this reaches you, Erik, know one thing: I want nothing to do with you. I only write because when we last crossed paths, I recall a babe in your arms. I do this for his sake. Chagny has found you. Leave. —Vahid.*

Erik lifted his eyes from the note to Philippe, and Simone's concerto for chickens. He didn't get a chance to address the pressure rising in his chest, for the second time in minutes his name rent the air. This time, it was personal.

"Anna?"

Philippe shoved off the fence. "Father, she sounded—"

Erik cut him off with one sharp slice of his hand. He knew what it sounded like—and it didn't seem pleasant. He lifted Simone from her rapt feathered audience and called Anna's name as he headed across the green toward the brook. He called her name again to no avail.

Philippe pointed to the ground as they approached the water and to the wet, dust-covered kerchief. "Whose boot prints are those?"

Erik's blood pumped harder counting the four sets of prints. "Go to Brother Lukas. Give him this." He thrust the note into his son's hand. "Tell him to pack my satchel, ready the horse, and do not set foot from the monastery."

"Why?" Philippe shook open the letter and read hastily. "What's going on? Who is Vahid? Where's Mother?"

Erik shoved Simone into Philippe's arms as he allowed his anger to billow. "Go now."

"Father, what?"

"Now!"

Philippe's curse and Simone's sudden whimper went unnoticed as Erik raced away. His focus was on the tree line and the perverse fury pumping through his body. If hatred were flames, the entire forest would be ablaze.

"*Anna!*" No response. Turning, he tried to grasp the direction they went. "*Anna!*"

He pushed through the thick brush. It would be so easy to give into the madness carving through the surface of his brain, allowing that part of him to rule the situation. But what of the promise he made years ago to Philippe de Chagny not to prostitute his anger ever again? A small tree bent and snapped. Erik growled and thrust it aside.

"Anna!"

Past promises could go to hell. No one would destroy what he had gained. Branches ripped as he tore a path through the woods. No one would rob him of Anna. Erik paused once in the clearing. A deadly silence surrounded him save for the noise in his head as he counted the dog and hoof prints. Noise he'd not heard in a very long time.

Erik stared through the trees. There was only one place he could go from here. Only one place where he knew he had allies.

The Opera Garnier.

The image of the opera house fogged everything in front of him as he tried to discern where Anna went. He saw the giant dome in each puffy cloud; every ray of sunlight that lit his path was the gild on the opera houses statues. The scent of the forest floor as his boots crushed rotted leaves reminded him of the mildewed aroma that permeated every crack and crevice of his hidden opera-house home.

He'd come to loathe the memories he had of the Opera Garnier. Life there had been an abyss of loneliness and a life plagued by dangerous obsessions. Breath heaving as he plowed through the trees, Erik fought to cling to the scent of Anna's hair instead. If he lost her…

Heart-shattering pressure rose in his chest at the thought of it.

Loup took her. Erik knew that more intimately then he knew his face and the terror and emptiness of that hurt more than if he were skinned alive. The thought of her fear pumped his blood hard, matching the throbbing headache his rising his madness always birthed in him.

A pain he'd not felt in years.

Raoul de Chagny, be careful what you steal from me.

Erik felt the destruction of that thought with every twig broken and branch he snapped. By the time he left the clearing and made his way through the village, the Phantom was watermarked on his every thought. He'd have taken off for Paris then and there, plundering the countryside with a wrath of a thousand armies if not for the image of Simone holding a bloody rock keeping him at bay. He had to make sure his children weren't out of their minds with fear.

Anna likely already was, and he was precariously close to losing his sanity too.

Erik's thoughts were finely aimed arrows by the time he reached his small house near the abbey. Once he got organized, he'd find Loup, and with him, de Chagny, then handle whatever consequences his rage dealt him after the fact. A quick survey of the yard confirmed that his horse stood at the ready, as did Brother Lukas. Erik clamped his teeth, making his headache even worse. Even though the dust swirling up from his angry strides made everything in his path look hazy, Erik could read the monk's worried caution.

He was in no mood for a holy lecture.

"Where are my children?" Erik huffed as he approached the cottage door. Brother Lukas was ready for him, bracing both his hands against the doorframe. "Lukas, either get out of my way or I plow right through you."

"You're not charging in there like a—"

"Madman?" Erik finished the sentence toe-to-toe with the monk. He glared down at him, using the good foot he had on Brother Lukas to his full advantage. Erik fought mightily to stay calm. It made his voice overly slow and his lungs heated. "I am beyond mad. I am livid, and every second you stand in my way is a second that my Anna suffers. Now, move!"

"I was going to say like an angry bull, Erik. The children are frightened and having you blow in there won't help."

"Then call down one of your almighty angels to hold me back."

Brother Lukas jumped away as Erik's hand came down over his shoulder and toward the door handle. Before Erik had a chance even to grip the knob, the door flung inward and his red-cheeked son barreled in-between him and the monk. The door slammed shut in his wake.

Philippe took five long strides past them before he whirled. His eyes were sharp and focused with the panic Erik refused to feel.

"Who is Vahid?" Philippe wasted no time in carving a figurative line in the sand.

"Where is your sister?" That only increased Philippe's pacing. He didn't take the bait of Erik's counter question.

"Where's Mother? What's going on?"

Erik's jaw set. This cursed manhunt was the one thing that birthed riddles for which he had zero solutions. But this time Erik was confident he knew the answer. He glanced in the direction of Paris. The church fire. The dogs. The man Simone swore sang *Alouette*. Despite what Erik knew in his gut, he was not about to tell his son that a ruthless huntsman just abducted his mother. He started toward the horse.

"Brother Lukas, take my son inside."

"I'm not a child, so stop treating me like one. Tell me what is going on."

Erik stopped short and shot his son a warning glance. As much as he wanted to grab the boy and convey to him that he understood, Erik was in a race between the noise in his mind and locating Anna.

Erik, slow down. The memory of Anna's voice calming him penetrated his mind and found momentary movement in his heart. Erik took a slow breath and stepped toward his son. He pointed toward the house and chose to focus on the one person Philippe could never resist.

"You need to go inside and mind your sister. She has been through enough today, and she is frightened." Erik attempted to leave again.

"Where are you going?" Philippe said, a slight waver to his voice.

The plea in Philippe's eyes was torturous. Unable to bear it, Erik turned to Brother Lukas instead. "I will be back before dark."

He stood there only long enough to watch the monk sag with the understanding that Erik had no intention of returning.

Not until he had Anna.

Erik spun his back to his son and didn't stop until he yanked the reins free from the hitching post. He paused once in the saddle, wrestling with the urge to leap off and reassure Philippe. He couldn't. The past was far too powerful and roaring in his mind with equal fervor. Driving the horse forward, he thundered out of the courtyard leaving the small home and children he loved in the dust. Erik hoped the monk would have the foresight to ask that God of his to forgive him for leaving his children alone and confused.

If forgiveness even existed. After all these years he still grappled with the concept.

The thought of Philippe de Chagny thumbed his way into Erik's mind. It and only forced him to ride the stallion faster, for Erik knew one thing and one thing alone.

Anna had been stolen from him, and he'd kill any man that laid a hand on her.

To hell with promises.

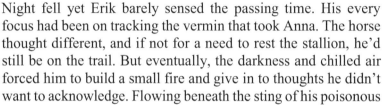

Night fell yet Erik barely sensed the passing time. His every focus had been on tracking the vermin that took Anna. The horse thought different, and if not for a need to rest the stallion, he'd still be on the trail. But eventually, the darkness and chilled air forced him to build a small fire and give in to thoughts he didn't want to acknowledge. Flowing beneath the sting of his poisonous anger was worry—a foreign feeling even after so many years of peace and kindness. Erik spent his life only worrying about himself until Anna, and her packages showed up. He couldn't fail her. That he'd lost her trail was a temporary set back; he had an absolute focus on getting to Paris.

He folded his arms and glared at the fire, feeling his hatred grow. If Loup touched her; if he dared violate her Erik would never forgive—

A curse shot out of his mouth, replacing that damned word "forgiveness." It echoed around the forest. Erik snapped a thin branch off a nearby bush and threw it down into the fire.

The crickets, with their happy melodies chirping around him, weren't helping his mood any. Simone loved crickets, and their song sank a knife further into Erik's heart. Philippe could manage without him. He may resent his father for leaving abruptly and dismissing his questions, a thought Erik tried to push away, but Simone wouldn't understand a wisp of this.

If on cue a thread of smoke trailed upward, making a lazy, carefree trail toward the stars. Erik refolded his arms to brace himself against the curl of smoke as if it had some power to penetrate his brooding. How long would Simone remain carefree in light of all this? And Philippe?

The thought of his son sent Erik pacing circles around the fire. That boy was too much like him. At some point, Philippe would put two and two together and figure out that Erik had a past best left buried. That this manhunt was rearing its ugly head was bound to get the boy asking questions.

Erik rubbed his temple—how he hated when Brother Lukas was right.

What was he doing pacing a fire? Erik shook off the thoughts and the stab of guilt for time wasted. He'd track Anna day and night from there on out and no longer give in to the need to *think*. There was nothing left to ponder besides finding her.

With that determination firmly in hand, Erik turned to his horse to grab the bladder of water Brother Lukas had provided in the saddlebag. As soon as the flames were extinguished, he'd press on until he had to rest the horse again.

His thoughts were heavy as he reached into the saddlebag and shoved his old cloak and hood to one side. Erik should give Brother Lukas credit for suspecting he'd need it. He felt a flutter of gratitude toward the old monk. Erik didn't want to have to wear that again, but there was no telling how Paris would greet him. He somehow didn't think it would be with a chorus of crickets.

Or with glowing eyes.

Erik squinted over the horse and through the woods. He knew that glow, and it kicked in a parental overprotectiveness he was still shocked he had. Erik ducked under the horse's neck.

"Simone?"

"Papa!"

Erik didn't have time to be surprised as she charged at him, not stopping until she landed against his hip. There was no way that child had made it this far into the forest alone at night, which only meant one thing. Erik's heart-racing protectiveness was replaced with clenched teeth as his son emerged from the woods. Erik's chest was nearly too tight to breathe, but he managed one carefully controlled word.

"Philippe."

His son squatted before the fire and warmed his hands. "I left a note behind for Brother Lukas." Philippe glanced from the fire up to meet his father's stare. "I wasn't about to stay behind. You should have known that I'd I learn a thing or two about tracking over the years."

The boy was fifteen going on fifty. Erik nudged his daughter off his hip and looked her over, head to toe. Her cloak was torn, and her cheeks smudged; she had a few leaves stuck in her curls, but she looked no worse for wear.

"Don't worry. She's fine, except for a few scratches on the arm not death-gripping your stupid violin."

So now his violin was stupid. Erik tried hard to govern his temper. Philippe's sarcasm and resentment were called for; he had to admit. Erik did abandon them right after their mother was abducted without the truth as to why.

"I am taking you back in the morning," Erik said, once convinced he could do so without sawing off his words. He would have marched them back immediately if not for Simone's yawning.

Philippe rose. "That will let whoever took her to get even farther ahead of us. You're not leaving us behind. She's our *mother*."

The firelight was enough for Erik to notice the dirt-smeared tracks of tears running over Simone's exhausted expression. Philippe had a point and had carried along with him enough guilt on a curly-haired platter to serve Erik for a lifetime. The village was the safest place for Simone, but something in Erik's gut told him that if he hauled his children back there, Philippe would only do something more drastic, like try to find Anna on his own.

Erik clamped down on his teeth and stifled a sigh. The fire he was about to extinguish would have to keep burning instead. As they burrowed down for the night, Erik rolled through memory after memory of camps just like this one. Except for this time

Anna was missing, and his violin wasn't silent. As Philippe paced the perimeter of the camp like a restless lion, Simone played a droll tune that highlighted the droop to her eyes. Her head kept knocking into Erik's arm as she began to nod off, so much so, he forced her to lower the instrument and curl into his lap. Though he tried to get Philippe to stop his restless patrol, the boy wouldn't listen. There was no point to Philippe's impatience. Loup was going to use Anna as a pawn to get him no matter how long it took for them to track her down.

There was one other distinct difference to this camp than from prior ones, Erik noted.

The Philippe that glared at him through the fire was going to be a far greater adversary than his namesake.

Throughout the night and on into the morning that thought had proved true faster than Erik realized. The dawn light intensified, slowly burning off the low fog that hung above the treetops. Leaning on the open cargo door and staring out at the countryside, Erik focused on the trees that whizzed past them as the boxcar sped down the tracks. The train belched steam and soon it was difficult to discern what was fog and what wasn't. He'd barely slept, in part because of Anna and in part because of oppressive guilt that weighed on him. This manhunt was already giving Simone a taste of the life he never wanted her to know. He had abandoned the horse at the first train station they came upon electing to ride the rails in the hope of faster passage to Paris. Some vagabond would come along and claim it. Erik always thought the first train ride his children would experience would have been in first class, not chasing down a moving boxcar and then jumping into its shadows.

Hopping trains and noisy boxcars, let along leaving behind a horse she adored, had turned Simone's music into a hodgepodge of notes. Confused one minute, low and dreary the next Erik listened without realizing that it matched his mood. It kept a sour taste in his mouth. Erik turned, as the music grew closer to him.

Simone stopped playing and lowered the violin once at his side. She stared out the boxcar door alongside him, a lopsided tilt to her head. He watched as she rapidly nodded as if observing a ball bob up and down. Erik glanced over his shoulder to Philippe as if he could decipher what had her so animated. The boy made it a point not to even look in Erik's direction. Instead, he stared out the opposite door, his back purposefully toward him.

"Simone," Erik placed a hand under her chin, "stop."

She looked up at him and without saying a word, lifted the violin, and began striking and whisking the bow across the strings in such a motion that the music blended in perfectly with the clacking of the rails and the wind that hissed past the doors.

Even Philippe turned around.

Folding his arms, unable to decipher the bizarre way the child transformed ordinary sights and sounds into music, Erik walked across the car toward his son. If he couldn't figure out what was going on in Simone's mind, he may as well try to unpack Philippe.

Erik instantly regretted it.

"Who is Vahid?" Philippe demanded as soon as Erik shared the opposite door. "You left him out of what you told me of your life at the Garnier, and yet he was the one who signed that letter. Now, Mother is missing. Who—is Vahid?"

The boxcar they stowed away on was already stirring Erik's memories and flaming his ire toward Chagny's manhunt. He wanted to snap his son off mid-sentence; the noise in his mind was building with each second Anna was gone. He grabbed Philippe by the scruff of the neck and gently turned him toward the other door.

"Calm your sister," he said; knowing full well he deserved the look of contempt Philippe shot him.

It was going to be an arduous trip to Paris.

"She doesn't need to be calmed down." Philippe stood, one foot planted toward his sister, the other toward his father.

"Trust me, Philippe, she does."

The boy turned his back to his sister and her violin, which every so often let out a wail perfectly mimicking that of the train whistle.

"A maestro is one thing," he said folding his arms and heading across the car toward Erik. His head was bowed, his stance like a trained barrister coming out for the cross. Philippe stopped at the open door again. "However, the Phantom of the Opera entirely another. Don't you think I should know everything? Why do you perpetually avoid my questions of this Vahid and how you came to be the Phantom?"

Erik pointed a finger of warning in the air between them, his voice harsh. "Be content to dwell on what I allow you to know."

"Which is practically nothing!" Philippe shouted, spreading his arms wide.

It was loud enough to make Simone end her clacking and whistling and lower her violin. She marched from her side of the boxcar, an annoyed look puckering her face. Mimicking what her father had done just moments earlier, she reached up on her tiptoes and laid a fingertip on Philippe's chin.

"Philippe. Stop." Plopping back down on her feet, she looked over to Erik. "You too.

A fog was growing in Erik's mind, and it was choking out his ability to think. He shouldn't be dragging his children into this, let along across Germany and into throes of all his mistakes. Erik reached over Simone and took his son's upper arm, forcing him to walk away. With a glance down to his daughter, Erik switched from German to French lest Simone understand anything more.

"Focus on the music," Erik said, calmer now for Simone's intervention. How long he'd remain that way was up to Philippe. "It will do you well. For some, music only births madness."

"Music speaks what words cannot in my opinion." Philippe challenged back, his French arrogant. "It has nothing to do with if a man is mad or not."

"It all depends on what you hear *behind* the notes." To have the chance to teach Philippe pure, unadulterated music was all Erik longed to do, but the music Erik heard wasn't pure, and his past, not something he wanted to let loose before his son. "You do not wish to know all that lies in my mind."

"*All* as in those tall-tales of the Phantom being a madman?" Philippe balked. "Is *that* what you are trying to say? You're no madder than Simone is truly daft."

Erik's clenched his teeth. Damn his loose tongue. He'd said

too much. "Simply repress her music."

"Repress her music?" Philippe thrust an arm back toward his sister who was zipping her head back and forth as she studied the trees zooming by. "That's like telling her never to speak again, which brings me to the point of why we're suddenly speaking French. What don't you want her to know?"

What didn't he want her to know? What a loaded question that was! He didn't want his children to know a thing about what was to come crashing down around their lives. Erik clenched a hand then loosened it trying to ebb his need to squash Philippe's curiosity. "Cage those—birds—of hers and ask no more questions of me!"

Philippe took a deep breath. "Father, if the de Chagny estate is looking for us—"

"Chagny!" Erik's voice boomed like thunder across the boxcar making Philippe flinch. Erik glanced at his daughter who blinked at him in equal surprise. Erik looked up and exhaled as she raised her violin and began mimicking the tracks again. He lowered his voice for her sake but punctuated his words with an air of angry warning. "Every last one of them can rot in hell. I will not have the life I finally command be a prisoner to the Chagny name again. I will not. I tell you, Erik will not!"

"*Erik* will not? Since when do you refer to yourself like *that?*"

Erik gnashed his teeth and wrestled down the noise rising behind the music in his mind. Philippe stared at him with a crimped face. Turning his back to his son, Erik walked closer to the opposite door. "I gave them everything when they left my opera house. Their lives, their liberty, and their love. Damn this all that I cannot have the same in return."

"Damn this all?" Philippe followed him to the door and stopped, sharing the same stance that Erik had. Tense. Angry. "Damn *you*, Father! My mother is abducted, my sister forced into a life she will *never* understand, you're telling me to stop the one thing she seems to adore, and you refuse to tell me every last thing I need to know to help! Let alone to understand!"

"You should not *have* to help! You should not have found out about us in such abrupt means. Mark my words, I will not allow my family to bear the scars of Chagny's obsession with me; it is bad enough that Simone already does!" He tapped his temple indicating the scab forming on her already marred temple.

Erik spun away, his angry strides putting distance between them and sending him to Simone's side of the car in a matter of seconds. His heart turned violently in his chest knowing he referred to much more than a blow from a rock. Simone's music shifted as he came to her side and ran his hands through her curls.

At least *she* could find joy in this situation. Erik's pain for what she didn't know at that moment could have yanked the sun down from the horizon.

SEVEN

Weeks being lugged across the countryside like one of Loup's dogs to end in this soul-sucking place added one more knot between Anna's shoulders. Paris' pre-dawn light shown through a high window of the small parlor, casting her shadow across an intricately designed marble floor. She watched her hand tremble via the reflection as she reached up to touch the back of her neck. Anna hissed.

Yanking her hand away, she glanced at her fingers. No blood, but her skin stung like a cat-scratched sunburn. Anna reached behind her head again to gingerly rub the base of her hairline where her scalp was left raw from the scrape of Loup's knife. She glanced to the door he'd gone through then down at her shadow once more. There was a mirror along the wall to her left, but she couldn't bear to look. Staring at the strange silhouette around her neck was shocking enough. Anna fought off exhaustion as she explored the rough edges of her hair that slid through her fingers. She pulled her hand away from her naked neck and with it a few loose strands. Wiggling her fingers, she watched the hair float to the floor. Wherever Loup had pranced off to, he took a piece of her with him.

His resounding laughter still bounced her ears. He had sliced her braid clear off, cropping her waist-long hair to her chin—preparation for her life in prison he had triumphantly announced, as he balled up her braid and shoved it into the pocket of his coat. Anna stopped pawing at her neck and dropped her arm to her side. Did Loup take her for a fool? She knew better. Her braid was his trophy, and where she stood wasn't any prison. It was a manipulative, grotesque way to toy with her mind. Like a cat playing with a mouse before the final pounce.

She studied the parlor, strategically avoiding the mirror and taking note of the familiar Chagny coat-of-arms hanging high above the doorway. The two footmen standing guard just outside the doors made bolting from this place impossible. Had there been a balcony she would have attempted to break a window and shimmy down a pipe with what the time and energy she had left, but she wasn't so lucky. She hated nobility and would have preferred a stone-cold cell to Loup raping her dignity and bringing her to the mouth of this lion.

Anna rubbed her eyes too tired to feel her usual disdain for Chagny. She slept little on the tedious journey out of Germany. Loup saw to that—in one awful way after another. She took a long, slow breath to center her thoughts and stared at the doors where the footmen stood guard.

I bet the comte will have a rude awakening this morning.

Anna circled a hideously posh armchair and tongued the inside of her mouth, prodding her bruised cheek. She didn't *want* to recall how she got that bruise, yet it was impossible not to. She didn't want to remember anything of the last several weeks, least of all Loup and his dogs. Anna shuddered.

Mother-of-God she hated dogs.

The thought quickened her heartbeat as she tried to shake off their barks and nasty wet-dog scent; or the way their jowls smacked together as they chewed their paws throughout the nights. Not to mention their unrelenting panting, no wonder Loup related to them; he was just as vile.

Anna stopped circling and shook out her hands, trying to toss away her fear. Now was the time to think, not stew over how she ended up in Chagny's Paris townhome. But thinking drew her mind in only one direction.

The children. They'd be frightened, and Philippe would channel that fear into a fierce determination to change things. But this manhunt and all the mysteries of the past were things that he couldn't change. Philippe wouldn't stop until he figured out a way to fix things and drive himself to the brink of his impulsive anger in the process. And Simone would... Anna scowled; she never could tell how Simone would process anything. What pieces of the puzzle were falling into place for her, if she even understood? They'd all understand soon enough, knowing Erik. Anna pressed her fingers to her temples. What mother does this to her children?

She followed a trail of dust traitorously highlighted by the early sun, up toward the window. Erik would descend upon Paris soon. The sense of him wound around her core and pulled at her as nothing else could. Anna glanced out the window and watched the sun start to light the streets of Paris. This pretty parlor, this quiet household, had no idea of the wreckage that was about to come. Erik would tear apart the city brick-by-brick to find her. If that wasn't chilling enough, Anna knew he'd begin looking where their past here ended, and the past reared an ugly head.

A crisply ironed paper was one of life's simple pleasures.

Like clockwork, his *maître'd* had it folded and ready for him at the table. Raoul smiled and nodded to the man standing stoically by the breakfast buffet as he took a seat at the table. Escaping to the morning paper and the scent of his cook's freshly baked bread was a welcome bit of routine during the happy chaos of a city always turned upside-down with one fantastic adventure or another. News of the Paris he loved filled the pages of *L'Epoch* and Raoul let his imagination take over. Paris was so different from the pace of Chagny. Despite the history it represented for him, he still adored his visits there.

"Good morning, Monsieur le Comte."

Raoul hummed a reply and ignored the way Legard styled

him. They'd become the closest of friends, and yet the man still insisted on convention. Raoul tapped the paper. "What do you make of this upcoming film, Legard? As if anyone could get to the moon." He shook his head and flipped a page. "Méliès will make a mockery of himself if he releases this."

Legard laid a plate of bread on the table. "So long as it doesn't cause a stampede when it releases, I'm fine with it."

Raoul lowered an edge of the paper. "Is there ever a time when you're are not thinking of protecting one thing or another?"

Legard shook his head.

"Is that the morning paper?"

Raoul glanced over his shoulder only long enough to watch André enter the breakfast room and see him scowl at the buffet table. As usual, he bypassed the plethora of choices and went straight to the urn of coffee. Unbelievable, that boy. Raoul shared a knowing glance with Legard. Chagny would one day be run on caffeine alone. Cup in hand, André took a seat at his side and nodded to the breakfast room door.

"How is *Maman*?" he asked.

Legard's voice held concern. "She looked poorly at dinner last night."

"She is well," Raoul explained. "Just wearing herself thin with all her visiting this trip. I suggested she take the day and shop."

"Shopping? She may never come up for air." André shared his father's chuckle and cocked his head to read the headline story sideways. "I've never seen such a fantastic—"

André's words were sliced thin as the door burst open. Raoul jerked his head to the sound so suddenly he felt a pull in his neck. He slapped the paper down on top of his jam-smeared bread and shot to his feet. Legard was already moving to the door.

"What are you doing back here?" Legard barked while Raoul's flustered *maître-d* raced to the door.

Loup sauntered in anyway, and Raoul had a sick, but excited feeling that he already knew why. He ordered his white-faced head-of-household back out the door, ignoring his apologetic look as Loup strolled past the buffet behind him.

"Why, good morning, Legard. You as well, Monsieur le Comte. Monsieur le Vicomte."

André rose, his voice tense. "Do you want me to see him out, *Père?*"

"Out? Why would your father want to see me out when I'm the one he's been looking forward to seeing the most?" Loup leaned back on the buffet and folded his arms. He was smug.

"You've been gone weeks. What's so urgent that you burst in here like a raving lunatic?" Raoul clipped, stepping out from his chair. Something inside of him always said to keep a clear path between him and his less than stable hunter.

"He *is* a raving lunatic," André muttered.

Raoul silenced his son with one lifted finger.

"You were ordered to return on one condition." Legard's voice held a slight hint of warning.

The thought of that condition heated Raoul's neck. "Have you any proof that Erik is in Germany?"

"Oh, I have proof," Loup smirked as he withdrew a long cord from his waistcoat and tossed it forward. It landed with a thunk on the headlines, bouncing bread across Raoul's plate.

"God's blood!" André shouted, leaping backward as the tail end of a long braid landed in his steaming coffee. "Is that—?"

"Anna's braid!" Loup laughed pushing off the buffet and leaning on the breakfast table. His head volleyed between Raoul, Legard, and André.

Raoul's entire body flashed hot this time at the deranged look on Loup's face. "What the hell have you done?" He nearly choked on his words.

"Nothing." Loup stood and straightened his waistcoat. He reached for André's cup, squeezed coffee-soaked hair back into it, and downed it in a swift gulp. The heat didn't seem to faze him. "Nothing except bring her here."

"Her? Mademoiselle Barret?" Legard's asked, a hint of disbelief riding his voice. "What do you mean you brought her *here?*"

"She's waiting in the morning parlor. Which is where I will be once you wipe that stupid look off your face."

Spinning on his heel, Loup pranced out the doors, the jaunty tune of *Alouette* following him down the halls.

André moved to follow, his face that wine-colored flush he always had when angry.

"Stay here," Raoul commanded. He allowed his son to know too much about the past already. He'd do all he could to keep him from entangling himself in the end of this manhunt, despite it being a part of André's life.

"The hell I will!" André stepped around the table, eyeing the braid as if it were a cobra coiled to strike. "Mademoiselle Barret is here which means so is the Phantom." He beat his father to the door.

Raoul wasn't going to have it. He knew things could quickly escalate from here, and the last thing he needed was a hotheaded sixteen-year-old overly anxious to be a man. "We know nothing. Stay here. That's an order and not a word to your mother."

Leaving André red-faced and fuming, Raoul's heart rammed hard in his chest. He'd put up with the bounty hunter's antics and drunkenness one too many times over the years. Raoul would take Loup out and rearrange the bones in his jaw for this stunt, if not for Christine. Her displeasure alone was going to be monumental. He hoped his wife stayed sound asleep for that matter alone as he followed Legard out the door.

So much for routine.

<hr />

I have to get to the Garnier!

As if Anna's thought had spurred the household into action, the parlor doors flung open and in bobbed Loup like a maniacal pied-piper.

"*Bon Matin, mon Alouette!*" He stopped inches before her and glanced to a small silver tray on a distant table. "Why, you've not touched your food; fine fare not to your liking? Perhaps you were expecting a pint of gruel and molasses, a bit of bread and some salt?" Loup flung himself into the massive wing chair she had been circling. "I thought it would be more fun to toy with you here rather than at a prison. The comte's shock was positively delightful when I informed him of this little stunt. Now I get to watch your pretty little body writhe in dismay at what may come next."

"I'm hardly dismayed."

"You might be hardly dismayed, but I'm definitely hard."

Anna flared her nostrils uncertain as to if it was revulsion or fear that flashed through her as Loup's hand shot out. He snatched her wrist and yanked her to him. Anna stifled a cry as her knees slammed against the floor. The momentum pitched her forehead forward, burying her face against Loup's obvious arousal. She yanked her head out of his lap.

His hand grabbed the sides of her jaw forcing her to remain in her submissive position. The flesh beneath his thumb and forefinger began to burn under his grip as her already bruised cheeks were marked with his fingerprints. Anna winced. He tilted her chin up slightly so their eyes could meet.

"Make my life easy while we are here, *Alouette*, and tell the comte what he wants to know. The sooner you do, the sooner you and I can be on to more delectable pursuits toward Belgium." He smiled. "Unless you're anxious to begin?" Loup's opposite hand reached for the buttons on his trousers.

Anna spat in his face.

"You whore!" He pushed her away, laughing as she landed flat on her back on the floor in front of him. He used his sleeve to wipe away her spit. "No time anyway, *Alouette*. You are about to meet some old friends."

A curt nod directed her attention to the sounds in the hall. She scrambled to get to all fours then her feet. A bonfire ignited in her belly as soon as Legard and the Comte de Chagny entered.

Anna rammed her teeth into her tongue. Years later and the sight of them could fold her skin inside out. A bitter taste flooded her mouth, and she fought the urge to spit it at their feet as she did Loup's face. The air in the small room, already unbearably stuffy, thickened.

"As soon as she tells me what I need you may contact the Belgian authorities," the comte said to Legard.

Anna's last meal threatened to reappear on her shoes. Not that it would be much. Loup was not exactly gracious in his care for her.

"Mademoiselle Barret, we meet again," the comte said, his voice taut.

She turned her back to him.

"It barely seems possible," he said incredulously. "Not even a month ago I was enjoying the opera and wondering if this moment would ever come. You've nothing to say?"

Anna stiffened as Loup stood and slapped a hand on top of her head. He twisted her around. Tight-jawed she watched the comte's expression harden at the sight of her. A huff jumped out her mouth. The bruises fading from purple to sickly yellow on her jaw would turn any stomach.

He should see the bruising Loup left on my thighs.

"Monsieur le Comte," she said, her voice monotone.

He tugged the immaculate sleeves of his waistcoat and strode further into the room. "I don't see the point in wasting words, Mademoiselle since you will be off to a trial shortly. Where is he?"

"Trial for *what*, Monsieur?"

That riled him. His look was indignant, as he wasted no time in answering. "Kidnapping, robbery, murder, aiding, abetting, arson." His brows shot up. "Do you have any idea what it cost me to rebuild the carriage house?"

Anna shrugged. "You forget. I stole your horse as well—a worthy and hefty crime."

He tried to contain his impatience but it leached out in the hole he attempted to wear in the marble floor. "Don't try my patience. Where is he?"

"Where is who?"

"I figured you'd be difficult. The Phantom. I suspect you have been with him."

"I know no Phantoms, Monsieur."

The comte looked at his boots, then up to the ceiling. A vein in his temple was bulging.

"Fine then, *Erik*."

"I've been alone for many years." Anna's speech was well

rehearsed, not that he could tell. "I was surprised you wanted me so badly." She looked at Loup. "But you obviously have your reasons."

"So you've no idea where he is?"

Anna tried hard not to roll her eyes as she continued to spoon-feed him her story. "We became separated a few months after the fire. I haven't seen him since."

"Was he to follow you?"

"I had no association with him after that. It was years ago. Perhaps Erik is with the diva. That's the way the story should be written, isn't it?"

The comte looked annoyed.

"Mademoiselle, I suggest you find the answers I need before I have you hauled off to prison. It will only be a matter of time before I transport you to Belgium. Legard. Loup."

Anna folded her arms and watched as the comte marched them out of the room. She kept her eyes upon all of them until they left, only slamming them shut when Loup blew her a kiss that sent ice down her spine. The door latched behind them, locking her in the most bizarre prison she had ever been in. Though the door deadened the sound, she could still hear the comte's voice clear enough.

"Have an eye on this room at all times. Alert the authorities and the theater police. Doubtful Erik is around as he has yet to be in any opera house, and he'd be a fool to show up here, but I'm not taking chances. I want all of Paris on this, Legard! And for the love of all things holy—get her downstairs and out of my parlor before my wife wakes."

There were a few indecipherable murmurs, the hasty shuffling of feet and a few silent seconds until the comte spoke again. His voice sounded even more strained.

"What did you do to her?" he said in a severe tone.

Anna seethed at Loup's laugh. As she heard their footsteps start to move away, she caught the first strands of a weariness color the comte's voice.

"Fetch my physician to tend to her jaw then get her out of there."

Her heart still raced, making Christine hotter than comfortable. The day started as lovely as could be. A good night's sleep dashed away her headache of last night, and her breakfast tray arrived in her chambers right on schedule. She indulged herself with a cup of hot chocolate instead of tea and ate her fill of bread and cook's sinful marmalade. There was a lively conversation with her maid as she dressed and Christine was looking forward to a wonderful Parisian day.

That is until she stepped outside of her chambers and caught wind of a different atmosphere. It didn't take long for her to uncover why. When she learned what the staff had been ordered to keep from her—she had little patience for Raoul's reasoning. There would be high water in hell before she did as he insisted and went shopping. She wasn't going anywhere until she had answers.

How? How could you do this to me, Raoul? Christine stared at the doors to the morning parlor mentally preparing to go inside. If Raoul found out she'd stormed off here leaving André waiting for her at their carriage, he'd surely tether her to his side. Well, let him try.

How could that woman be in my home and not an appropriate prison? How could he permit this injustice to the Chagny name?

The two burly footmen stationed on either side of the door didn't glance at her, and if they had, Christine would have leveled them with one of her own—just as she did her husband after letting him know how displeased she was to discover Anna Barret was here. And in her parlor of all places! Raoul fed her some excuse that he'd ordered his physician for the woman and then she'd be relocated below stairs. That man and his overly sensitive heart! Christine didn't care, her house was being disgraced, and it was her husband's fault.

Anna Barret is in my home!

Subconsciously her hands fluttered about her dress as if

preparing to meet a queen, not her nemesis. It had become a habit for her to hide her nerves that way. She'd allow herself time to fidget right before taking the stage for a big aria. This was no different. Funny how she wasn't convincing herself that is was. She tried to align nerves in some sort of order.

Christine stared at the doorknob. If that woman was here, then so was that hunter. She shook as a chill ran down her spine. Raoul may be at fault for keeping Anna in her home, but it was that awful beast Loup who delivered her. She'd give up the stage to never see that man again. Loup had a way of rendering her powerless.

Perhaps it was his blackmail and all the secrets she'd been keeping from her husband that made her shake instead.

Swallowing the fear Loup's name evoked, she breathed deeply and laid a hand on the knob. She'd heed Raoul's suggestion to shop around Paris only after Mademoiselle Barret looked her in the eye and told her where Erik was.

Keeping his name tucked under her heart and using it to bolster her confidence, she twisted the knob and glided into the parlor. As the door closed behind her, Christine scanned the room, spying Anna staring out a window to the courtyard below.

"Mademoiselle Barret," she addressed, somehow knowing Anna wouldn't pay her the appropriate respect and address her first. "We meet again."

When she turned, Christine gasped.

Merciful God! The shades of green and purple on her cheek explained the physician. Christine swallowed back a nasty taste and forced herself to continue. "Your tenure at my home is only by the graces of my husband. I'm told you'll be sent to prison soon. I can't say this upsets me, given what you have placed my family through over the years."

Anna didn't look surprised. Christine couldn't register anything on the woman. It was as if it didn't matter to her at all what she had said. It was likely an act, Christine decided.

"I've placed your family through nothing," Anna replied. "Any perpetuation of this affair is due to your lies."

Indignant, Christine took a few steps toward her and stopped.

"How dare you speak of me." She followed Anna's steady gaze toward the window and the carriage that waited in the courtyard below. Christine noted her eyes were on André as he patiently stood near the horses.

"Is he yours?" Anna asked quietly.

Caught off guard, Christine watched her son momentarily before discovering the first readable expression in Anna's eyes. She looked sad.

"My son. André Thaddeus Marie, the Vicomte de Chagny. He just turned sixteen."

"Quite the man already."

The frankness to her voice dumped rocks in Christine's stomach. She jutted her chin to the ceiling and tried to ignore them. Whirling in front of the window, she blocked Anna's view of the courtyard. "Don't you dare speak of my son! I'm well aware of the murder you committed against the house of Molyneaux, and I'll not have the likes of your eyes upon my child." As a puff of air broke through Anna's lips, Christine laid a hand on her tumbling rocks and quickly changed the subject. She didn't like the idea of standing in front of a cold-blooded murderer. "My husband has informed me you've been alone. That you've no idea where Erik is, and you haven't seen him in years."

"I haven't."

Truth or lie? Christine couldn't tell, but secretly she hoped it was the truth. It would give her jealousy a break from churning in her belly. "I can't say that surprises me, Mademoiselle Barret. The Phantom follows no one. He's a man of particular taste." The look that flared behind Anna's eyes gave her a renewed courage and strength. Christine took her hand off her churning stomach and, seeing as she struck a chord, propped it on her hip. "You threw your life away hoping for his love, you know. Helping him escape the opera house, thinking he'd return that favor by loving you. I hope you've not wasted these years thinking about why you did that. You can never understand the depth of the Angel of Music and how he loves. Not as completely as I do."

Anna moved around her toward the window, forcing Christine to turn with her. "Is he his?" she asked nodding to the courtyard.

Christine's eyes shot open wide. The nerve! "Of course not!"

Anna's tone spit bullets through the windowpane. "Then I will stand here and remember with a silent and private satisfaction the passion involved the night *your* Angel of Music created *my* son."

Frozen by the implication, Christine stood as ridged as the footmen on guard outside. Inside, however, she was melting, and her blood flowed cold as ice.

She lied. The Angel of Music was a presence rooted in *her* soul, not this harlot! Erik would never take another under his wing. "You speak wicked lies, Mademoiselle. Erik would never have chosen you over me."

"Is that so?"

Christine gasped. The woman was delusional. "You seek to vindictively destroy him for some reason like you do my family. Stand there—be as arrogant as you want. Refuse to tell us of his whereabouts; it matters not. Your association with him ends with a carriage to Belgium where you can take your lies with you."

Anna whirled her back to the window and stared Christine in the eye.

"My association ends?" she said, as Christine watched her chest start to heave. "So long as my son lives and breathes the very essence of the man you so ardently claim to be yours; so long as my daughter sees the world through the golden eyes of her father and the fair-haired curls that were my mother's, my association with him will *never* end! Erik is *my* inspiration, *my* blessing, and *my* soul, and I would appreciate it if you didn't speak of *my children!*"

Christine took a step backward, her hand clutching the cameo at her collar as Anna stepped closer. "I'm well aware of the lies *you* committed against your own house to perpetuate your ridiculous jealousy of me, and I'll not have you wish for one moment longer that Erik wants any part of *you!*"

Christine stared at her so stonily she thought her heart was too heavy to resume beating. She backed her way toward the door. "Liar. This will all be over soon. As soon as you are locked away forever, everything will be as it was."

Christine fumbled with the doorknob and gasped when it finally sprung open, giving her the freedom to breathe. She didn't look back to the parlor as she raced through the hallways. The walls seemed to be closing in on her. Christine barely acknowledged the servants tending to her cloak and bonnet once she made it to the courtyard door. She fled through them to the courtyard below and didn't stop until her shaking hand was resting in the firm grip of her son. Only once he assisted her into the coach did she look up toward the parlor window.

Anna's silhouette would haunt Christine almost as much as her untruths.

EIGHT

His timing was off.

The morning was not when Erik had wanted to arrive in the city outskirts. Moving with caution through the alleyways and channels of a city just waking was far easier when he was a Phantom. Doing so with two alert children proved challenging. He kept his head down and hood up taking care to conceal his mask. He took no chances. With his legacy pounded into Paris tighter than the cobbles under his feet, Erik doubted such a city would have forgotten him after so many years. Philippe and Simone flanked him, a complete contrast from the last time he wove his way through the back alleys of the city, angry, shot, and on the run.

"Is this really Paris?" Wonder filled Philippe's voice.

Erik yanked him by his collar back into a shadow for the fifth time. This *was* Paris—but not the Paris he remembered. The extraordinary had taken over his city and a carnivalesque atmosphere hummed around him like mad bees in a hive. People swarmed everywhere. Fantastic displays, an inventor's dream, lined the streets at every turn. Performers roamed with outstretched hands like hungry minstrels searching for fresh ears. Great new buildings rose as if coming from Atlantis itself, and the entire world seemed to lie at Paris's feet. Rising to the sky far in the distance was an abomination Erik had never seen; a massive tower that jutted from the streets to the heavens. Curiosity bellowed at him to explore the transformation of his beloved realm. With so many roaming about lost in the bustle of it all, no one would notice Erik, but he refused to take a chance.

Philippe spun with almost every step he took. Any anger he harbored had, for the moment, been set aside for wonder. The aromas of sidewalk cafés and bakeries, the sounds of hooves on cobbles were all foreign to his children as was the din of Parisians as they hustled to and fro. Awe-worthy buildings and fantastic places greeted Philippe at every corner, and out of the three, he was the only one capable of blending in. If he could, Erik would have fostered this delight in his son, but he had more pressing things on his mind.

Mainly attempting to breathe.

Simone clung to his neck as tightly as she could, horror-struck at the activity of the city. Her one hand not grasping the violin and bow was clamped tightly over her normal ear. She whimpered over the sounds complaining the cobbles chattered louder than her birds. Shifting her, Erik lifted the hood of her cloak over her face.

"How will we find Mother in all this? How do you know for sure she is even here?" Philippe's query was an invisible slap across Erik's face.

He didn't know. It was an assumption that just made sense. The manhunt started here, likely it was meant to end here. They'd followed Anna's trail for weeks, asking whoever seemed trustworthy if they'd seen a woman of her description with a man of Loup's. When the trail led farther from Chagny and closer to Paris, Erik became more confident. Finding her wouldn't be easy. He'd need help, and one problem stood in his way.

He'd learned long ago that misfortune had met with Madame Giry, the old box keeper, ending in her demise. She was his one true servant in life, and now she was gone. Had circumstances been different he would have kept in contact with her more through the years, and her death was a painful stab in the heart.

Knowing she was an ally in Paris, should he ever have to return, had been a salve to what he put Anna and Philippe through during the manhunt. What to do with his children now? He wouldn't have them wait in the Garnier while he avenged Anna's kidnapping.

There was a part of Erik that was a natural survivor, and he focused on that problem instead of his son's intense questions. Fate had returned him to Paris, but it didn't have to drag his children into the sewers with him. With Madame Giry watching him from the heavens there was only one other place he could go, and hell was not an option.

"Whatever you do, do not move from this stoop," Erik instructed. Looking up and down the road he was satisfied they were safely tucked out of sight. "Wait here until a man either comes out of that door or enters it. He will have jade eyes and an annoying sense of fashion."

Erik had no idea of the Persian's current habits. Not like in the past when he was as a boil festering in his life—always there and just barely about to burst. This was the last place he wished to deposit his children, especially with Philippe's questions, but it was better than bringing them to the belly of the beast. Until he had a chance to calm the rising noise in his mind, Philippe and Simone were better off far away from the Garnier, and Erik best off far away from the Daroga of Mazendaran.

Without Anna's guidance, he was not half the man he could be.

"Stay here?" Philippe gasped wrapping an arm around Simone's shoulder as she buried her face in his hip. "I'm not staying on some corner like a street rat, Father. We're going with you."

"Do I as say."

"Do as you say when I've no idea what I'm to do?"

Erik looked at Simone, his mask suddenly feeling like it weighed a ton. "What you are to do is to keep your sister safe." He replied in French, causing Philippe to cuss under his breath.

"Keep her hood up, her face away from everyone. Do not allow her to play that violin do you hear me? Not one note! This place will only do her harm and I cannot, I will not—Philippe!" Erik grabbed his son's shoulders and shook him sternly. The noise in his mind was like shards of glass wiggling their way through his skull. "Please," he pleaded. "Just do as I say until I–"

"Until you *what*?"

One glance from the persecution behind Philippe's crystal blue eyes to Simone's golden ones was all Erik needed to set him over the edge. The choice was simple. Stay and wrestle his rising demons in front of them, or retreat until sane enough to reason? Grabbing his son's cheeks in both his hands he searched his eyes, ignoring the way he squirmed and scowled. If Philippe continued to challenge him, he would crumble like rubble and spare no detail to his brilliant heart. Was it worth the risk to lose his love forever?

Erik released his son as if he became a hot rock and vanished into the Paris streets. The city would have no idea who it swallowed. The voice of a master ventriloquist swirled around his children as he disappeared into shadow.

"Vous savez je t'aime."

It was all Erik could do to hope his children knew he loved them.

He kept that thought thrumming in his mind as best he could as he left them standing there. It wasn't easy to do. Memories bombarded Erik with each step he took. Memories that mingled with the sounds in his mind and threatened to tear him apart with madness or desperation. He retraced steps which years ago he wore like a second skin. Paris had once been his to command when he permitted himself the luxury of leaving his tomb. Shadows had cloaked him all his life, so melting into them now and flowing through the streets was second nature. All of Paris had its attention elsewhere, yet his focus was narrowed like a hunter in quest of his meal.

His search of the magistrate and the prisons turned up empty. Even as a wanted man, he arrogantly prostituted his talents enough upon unsuspecting street urchins willing to find him information for a bit of coin. Though he should be grateful she was not locked in some dank cell; he was not. Erik fought a twisting disconnect from the world around him each time he met with a dead end. It built and built with each stone he unturned only to find Anna not there.

Now fighting the rising noise in his mind, he scurried like a rat away from his children and shunned the light of day until the familiar catacombs seeped their dampness back into his bones. There'd be no way Anna was here, but Erik had to return to either gather his thoughts or give in to them. If he scrambled back to his children in this state he was uncertain as to what he'd do. The pain the darkness created was old and familiar. The only rays of light he clung to were those last words he spoke to his children. The bottomless black reaches far below the Opera Garnier which had once provided him with peace and respite, still had the power of birthing a cavernous hole in his heart. Nothing made him feel more hollowed then losing his Anna and leaving his children behind to wonder who, or what, their father had become.

What Erik became, was angry.

Eerily, as if waking from a still dream, he looked beyond his anger to see everything was as he left it. Arriving on the banks of the underground lake, Erik discovered the boat still stood where he last moored it. If he closed his eyes, he could recall Christine stepping from it as vividly as he could remember Raoul's bullet tearing through his arm. Erik swore if he looked down, scarlet would be coating his sleeve.

The boat had not held up over the years but served its purpose without sinking. After a silent row across inky blackness that should have saved his senses, he docked at the entrance to his drawing room. The single candle he swiped from an office above was his only light until he got more candelabras lit. Such wasn't easy. Old wax doesn't burn well.

He had forgotten how quiet it was, how oddly beautiful too. As the light grew and his eyes adjusted to the soft glow, Erik surveyed his domain. It held up to a degree over the years, surprisingly surging relief through his veins. Everything was still damp and cold, and rats had found their way into his scores.

Somewhere in this labyrinth was a very musical nest.

Dangerous notes tripped through his mind. He crept toward the organ lining the wall, to his chambers as if it were the forbidden fruit. Reaching out Erik touched the cold metal pipes. Rust coated his palms. He continued his inspection stepping gingerly over the remnants of a past rage, to the room beyond, lighting candles he passed.

The memories of his last moments down here swirled like the mist on his lake. He remembered cradling Christine in his arms as he and lay her down in the Louis-Philippe room, recalling how nervously he waited for her to wake, and in the confrontation that followed, how drastically his life had changed.

Erik stared intently at the coffin standing in the center of the room on a small platform. Feeling his pulse throb in his neck, Erik fought the head-on collision of his past and the present. He closed his eyes to the memory of sleeping in that choosing instead to evoke the various makeshift beds he shared through the years with his Anna: hay one night, a bedroll the next; If lucky and not in an area known, perhaps warm linens in a local tavern. Tuning everything out, he listened. The only sound he heard was the distant yet comforting lap of water against the shore outside as it wrestled for a spot next to the building noise in his mind. In essence, it was the heartbeat of his womb. Opening his eyes, they roamed over the red brocade fabric hanging over the coffin to read the stave of the *Dies Ires* on the wall. Several stories above him was an opera house living in silent oblivion to his return and a city unprepared to meet the rage that was exploding within him. One second longer without Anna—the pacifier his madness—and Paris would reverberate with a Phantom they had never met. The theater was clueless about the thoughts in his head, ignorant to the woman he missed, and unaware of the titled man he sought to kill.

Kill.

That single word jolted him as if lightning struck from the blue. Erik's face contorted beneath his mask. With his body twisting into the memories, he fought the image of Philippe Georges Marie, Comte de Chagny from his mind. Struggled to shove aside the memories of his only friend and the life he insisted he lead beyond that of a Phantom. But like ghosts, those memories floated around him, passing through things on their way to penetrate another. Everywhere he looked he remembered Philippe.

With noise tangoing with the music in his mind, he left his chambers and absently studied his house with new regard. How had he ever lived down here? No sunlight, no children laughing, no one sharing his bed. He caught sight of himself in one of the still shiny pipes of his organ and chanced to look out of the corner of his eye. Mirrors, no matter the sort, were implements of pain and none existed in his life since Anna. The only reflection he needed to see of himself was the one in her eyes. He looked anyway at the rounded and distorted figure.

His mask was seamless with the ebony of his dress and blended in beautifully with his clothing. Though he looked nothing like the maestro of his past, his finer clothing shed long ago for a life on the run; he still portrayed an odd elegance. He took a good, hard look at that reflection, unable to tear his eyes away. He arrived a carpenter, desired to be a maestro and still reflected a Phantom.

With a shout that echoed vehemently across his home, Erik's arm cut across his body, clearing the contents of a nearby table. Old ink bottles, blotters, nibs, and paper scattered through the air. Every emotion possible came rushing upon him as he stared at himself in the pipe. The reflection mocked him; it wanted something of him, making him grasp the side of the table until his pallid knuckles went whiter. Memories, once reopened can sting if allowed. An urge to unmask time and expose it for the cruel judge it was rose in him to the point he could no longer govern man verses madman. He suddenly felt the need to distance himself from the labyrinth. He had to, lest he unleashed those maddening notes on Paris and Anna was made to suffer. He needed to be near those who didn't know a Phantom.

He needed his children.

Erik never left the house on the lake so quickly.

⇒ •·————···————··• ⇐

Droplets of rain dappled the dark fur on his Astrakhan hat. The dawn had looked promising, but now, bah, he hated the weather in France. Head bent against it; he cursed the disgusting slurry of mud coating his boots and soaking the hem of his trousers. If it were going to rain, he'd rather a sudden soaking downpour than this annoying hovering mist that clung to everything. A simple trip to satisfy a craving at the local patisserie had turned into an affair that took hours. He had lingered far too long attempting to avoid the weather, the only good coming out of it was the second helping of a poppy seed tart. Like any other caught in this mess, he wanted to arrive home, pour something strong, and settle down in the warmth to regard Paris in a more comfortable light.

The streets were crowded with businessmen and young lovers hastening to shelter, or foreigners craving more excitement, making Vahid dodge and weave his way toward his flat. The closer he got to his home, however; the streets began to clear. Such was unusual near the Tuileries, for the gardens drew crowds no matter the weather. Curious, he slowed his steps. Braving getting wet, he stopped, scowling at a distant crowd gathered in the vicinity of his building's door.

Instinct kicked up an uneasy feeling in his gut. Spending years as the chief of police to Persia's Sultana, he had a wariness for crowds. They usually didn't bode well, especially not on a misty Paris morning. Nothing he could think of would make any traveler stop in their efforts to get home, but then again, this was Paris.

Until he heard the music.

A low, mournful tune forced his feet forward. The lone strands of a violin wept through the air matching the muffled mood of the rain. The closer he got, the more mesmerized by the melody he became. Heads in the back of the crowd craned to catch a glimpse of the violinist as curious onlookers braved slipping on the tips of their toes to see.

Another wandering troubadour begging for some coins, perhaps?

Several in front of him swayed slowly, matching the seductive sounds. Occasionally, the distinct clicks of coins hitting what cobbles were not covered in mud poked through the weeping notes. Whispers rippled through the crowd of the child's magnificence on the strings.

Child?

The crowd was several deep making Vahid shoulder his way forward. When the music slowed and almost stopped, applause filled the air. As if the encouragement were a cue to change the feeling behind the piece, so turned the music. So sudden was the shift; it jolted Vahid like scorpion's sting.

Spinning, rising, and skipping through the air the melody became a wild and lively adventure. The crowd clapped in rhythm to the tune. Awestruck chatter replaced curious whispers, and soon even the downtrodden and wet were tapping their feet to match the music. Finally, in a position to see, Vahid froze.

For all the...

A child danced in the streets—whirling madly in the mist. A large cowl covered her features, but the ends of blonde curls poked from either side of the hood. She bowed and swayed, leapt and laughed in tune with the music pouring from her violin. The music possessed her and with it, the crowd. Wide-eye he watched her dance, awe-struck that he would never see such a sight nor hear such music outside of Paradise. The tune became livelier with each note, and with it her dance. A dramatic bow followed by a grand leap that threw notes careening across the crowd, also sent her hood flinging off her head.

The rain speckled her crown of gold. The dance spun her round and round. The still-lit street lamp above her illuminated a hideous face of Death with every revolution she made. Vahid ducked the sudden clamber of noise. Women screamed. Men twirled their wives away. Children cried. The little girl, oblivious to it all, played on.

Motionless in the commotion, Vahid allowed one minute for fear to knife him. At that moment he knew three things: this was no ordinary progeny, her deformity wasn't the result of an accident, and his life was about to change.

While the crowds ran in the opposite direction, he ran forward, scooping the startled child into his arms. The music abruptly stopped and her voice, just as penetrating rent the air, nearly halting the rain in the sky. Ignoring her flailing legs and the crazed language falling from her lips, he rushed her inside before the police came to investigate.

And they would investigate. The evidence in his arms proved Vahid's worse nightmare had come true.

Erik had returned to Paris, and this time he wasn't alone.

···············

Even the back streets were in their own right, seductive. Philippe would have given in their allure if not for the nest of snakes in his gut. Worry grew constant as seconds ticked off into minutes, minutes into hours, hours into days and then into weeks since his mother was abducted. If he knew all the whys of the matter, the churning wouldn't be so great. Philippe's mind was a delicate instrument, soaking up every detail it could and storing it away for future recall. But in the matter of his family's history, his details were as spotty as water on silk.

Slicking back the mist from his hair, he quickened his pace. Leaving Simone for even a second didn't sit well with him, but after three hours of her insistent pleas for something to eat, Philippe caved. All it had taken was a flash of his smile; a flex of a sculpted arm and an irresistible wink to make the young mademoiselle at the pushcart practically shove the bread at him. His heavily accented French and the seductive lilt he could place in it didn't hurt. At least he learned a few things from his father.

Blowing out his mouth and watching his breath coat the air, he fought down the urge—again—to follow his father. He crammed the bread under his coat lest it got soaked.

He knew enough of the past to know his father would head to the Opera Garnier. After all, isn't that where this manhunt started? Philippe figured the mysterious opera also held the answers to a lot of other questions he had. Like the tales around the Phantom of the Opera and who this Vahid person was. He looked around wondering what direction the opera was in. What he didn't understand was his father's passionate reaction to anything relating to madness. It made no sense.

The idea of his father actually being mad only knotted those snakes tighter. Rounding the corner onto the street where he had left his sister, he stopped in his tracks the instant he saw the empty stoop.

"Simone?" Mud smeared the street as if a mob had gathered. Philippe's heart pounded. "Simone?"

No reply.

He saw her tiny boot prints everywhere and one large set that led straight from the center of the fray up the steps and through the doorway on which they'd been deposited.

Philippe dropped the bread.

Two strides and one sharp butt of his shoulder had him through the door and with him, his panic.

Taking the flights of stairs two at a time, Vahid rushed into his apartments not caring to shut the door behind him. Winded, he plunked the girl down in the center of the room and paced in circles, myriad curses falling out his mouth. As soon as the child's feet hit the floor, she burst away from him in a tiny explosion of feet and hair. Vahid, arms akimbo in shock, stared slack-jawed at the table she clambered upon.

"Wake up you old fool, wake up! This isn't happening. I'm dreaming. I had too much aperitif last night," he muttered to himself. Now on a level plane, the girl twirled to face him. Haunting golden eyes met his green ones. This was a nightmare never mind a dream.

A soon as he caught his breath and wits, he studied her tip-to-toe. The sour taste of a tart crept its way up his throat. He swallowed his revulsion and chastised himself. *Stop, Vahid! She is just a little girl! Fate, you are a cruel servant to mark her in such a way!*

He tipped his head to focus on the small scrap of her face not marred by the mark of being Erik's kin. That patch of youthful skin, which stretched down to a ruby pout, combined with her crown of curls, would have made for the picture of innocence. He didn't realize he stared, but the child did. She shrank, one small hand wrapping over the hideous part of her face. His heart panged in pity at that simple gesture.

"No, it's all right," he comforted. Gingerly, he raised a fist to his mouth. An intriguing offspring of the onset of shame was shyness, but one thing was certain; if this was Erik's child, she wouldn't be shy.

"*Guten Tag*," she greeted springing her hand free, yanking him from his thoughts.

Startled, Vahid shook his head clear. Her voice had the power to melt his bones in ecstasy, yet at the same time, it pierced him.

"Tell me little one," Vahid cleared his thoughts as nonchalantly as he could. "Where might your father be?"

The girl pouted. She hugged the violin harder against her chest and shook her head.

"Ah," Vahid realized. "You don't speak French. Perfect."

"Get away from my sister!"

Officially a nightmare. Vahid spun around. His first impulse was to lash out at the intruder in his doorway, but that sentence, executed in perfect French pinned him to his spot. The young man filled the space, his height dwarfing Vahid and his shoulders nearly reaching from frame to frame. He was the complete opposite of the girl on his table. As deformed as she was, he was flawless perfection.

Reaching up, Vahid removed his hat and tossed it on a nearby chair.

"Your sister? Allah have mercy." He rubbed his stubble as if the action would clear his head of the idea Erik had a son.

"Allah?" the boy echoed. He studied Vahid in a way that made him uncomfortable, then looked around the room as if taking in every last artifact. "You are Eastern. A Persian?"

"That all depends on who desires to know." The boy made his way toward the girl. He even moved like Erik. He could feel beauty and command pour out of the steps he took.

"You didn't answer my question," the boy replied.

"You didn't answer mine."

"Kidnapping is a crime you know."

"Really? Tell me, young man, did you learn that from your father—"

"Daroga!"

Stopping mid-retort, Vahid snapped his mouth shut as the world came to a screeching halt. He turned to his door, moving as if swimming through mud. To his astonishment, though he shouldn't have been surprised at all, he stared face-to-face with the black-masked nightmare of his past. The only happy person in the room was the child bubbling like a teakettle on the table. Erik took immediate command, his eyes never leaving Vahid's. He walked directly to the table and plucked up the girl, whose demeanor lit up the room as if it were the sun itself that walked through the door.

Far too comfortable for Vahid's liking, Erik sat in his hearthside chair, the child curling up in his lap. The tall youth quickly took a spot at his side completing the most bizarre family portrait Vahid had ever seen. He raised a salty eyebrow and asked the question he swore he never would.

"What are you doing here, Erik?"

"Taking my children to the gardens, Daroga. Why do you think I am here?"

Erik's veneer of sarcasm was never forgotten. It had an odd way of cracking the tension in the room. Vahid approached and hesitantly extended his hand. It took a moment before their forearms clasped in a wary truce. He hid his surprise at Erik's touch. He had forgotten how cold he was.

"Vahid," Erik stretched his long fingers in a gesture to the young man to his side. "My heir, Philippe Georges Marie."

The youth's expression had gone from sour to surprised, and if Vahid wagered a guess, that look held a thousand questions. Vahid only had one he dared not voice.

Whatever reasons you chose for christening that boy after the former Comte de Chagny, I'm certain I don't want to know. Mind your tongue, Vahid. Mind your tongue! Nodding a silent greeting to the boy, he looked at the child in Erik's arms.

"My daughter, Simone."

Bewildered, Vahid shook his head. "Then I am—charmed?"

Erik cocked his head. "Do not expect the same of her. Simone elects not to speak much lately unless it is through the violin."

The girl had tucked the instrument under her chin and was a tapping the strings with the bow. If a violin could say it was impatient to be played, then this one screamed it.

"Through it?" Vahid swallowed. He needed a drink. A stiff, stiff drink.

"She has my more—expressive side."

"Delightful."

"Philippe is the genius."

The boy's stare penetrated him to the marrow. Floored and making no attempt at hiding it any longer, Vahid raised his hands and backed away trying to erase the scene before him. "I simply am not seeing this."

"Yes, Daroga, procreation. I discovered I rather like the process."

A light mist continued to fall forcing a chill into the evening air. Though cold and damp, Erik insisted they speak outside safely away from the children. Dinner had been a lively event, mostly an intricate sidestep of Philippe's questions, which they had managed to focus for the most part on the history of the opera house. The balancing act was between Simone and her curiosity of the dark-skinned man. Her music had taken on a strange, exotic feel. While Erik perched himself on the balcony railing and stared off at the warm glow of Paris, Vahid looked opposite, into flickering lights of his townhome. In the distance, Simone moved like a snake charmer, filling his house with music he had not heard since he left the sands of his country. How she did it, he dared not ask.

"Never would I have expected this out of you, Erik."

"I thought this is what you wanted out of me, Daroga."

"It's not a complaint. I'm just surprised. It's been years since we saw each other and a great deal has come to pass in that time. This is a complete concurrence to the stories I've been hearing." He tossed the remnants of a fig into a potted tree. The seeds were unusually annoying tonight. "Seeing you with children is odd. You're the Phantom of the Opera, after all. It's—peculiar."

Very few men were not unnerved by the night's ability to make Erik's eyes glow their yellowed hue. The daroga didn't flinch under the severity of his glare.

"I am a man like anyone else, Daroga."

There was something to his tone that made Vahid down his sarcasm. "Philippe is captivating. I hope I live long enough to see that young man's untapped genius surface. There's no doubt he has a passion for the opera house. In a much better way, than you did, I might add." Glancing over his shoulder, Vahid noted Erik's regard was clamped on the dome of the Garnier.

"He will command a world I never knew."

Vahid's brow inched up at Erik's unfathomable statement. He followed his strange friend's glance back toward the townhome.

"There is not a door that will not be opened to him; no opportunity denied, no rejection whatsoever. He is perfect." Erik's voice was distant.

A small, and what Vahid perceived as a proud, smile moved across his thin, misshapen lips. Never in his years had he seen the monster smile.

"And the girl?"

"What of Simone?"

"One cannot help but notice she is a bit unusual. Is she…?" Vahid tapped his temple.

"Mad?"

"Not the word I was looking for, but given that she is your child—"

"She is a little girl, Vahid. She likes flowers and crickets and has a fondness for the night. She is capable of concepts of beauty beyond your understanding, her imagination vivid and sharp! There is a genius in her as well. She has no concept of destiny or fate, cruelty or hatred, rejection or betrayal. No concept of the ugliness that rests in the hearts of men!"

Opening his mouth, Vahid tried to interject, but a fuse ignited in Erik that burned for much longer than their conversation.

"She is a little girl who understands, for now, a *compassionate* world. And Erik intends to keep it that way as long Erik possibly can!"

Pursing his lips, Vahid kept silent. It never was a good sign when Erik began to refer to himself in the third person. The monster of madness woke and was rumbling to the surface. Erik's voice shook the potted palms, yet Vahid remained unmoved.

"You great booby! How dare you pass judgment?" Erik slammed a fist into the railing. It shook behind their backs. "How dare you label my daughter as mad?" Only when Vahid raised his hand in defeat, did Erik soften his tone. He sounded much like a wounded child. "She is the very beat of my heart, Daroga."

Erik turned away as a flare of light below them broke the night. He watched the lamplighter in silence until Vahid found his voice. He turned to regard Paris along with Erik and pressed his forearms against the cold railing. "Over several years I've been contacted by Inspector Jules Legard. He is Chief of Security for the Chagny estate now. There's quite a manhunt going on for you."

"Well aware, thank you."

"You murdered some men? That's what started his pursuit?"

"Man."

"That's not what the authorities say. They claim you killed three people and burned down the opera's carriage house."

"Anna's father, Richard Barret, killed the managers Laroque and Wischard. I saved Anna *and* Christine by killing Barret, delight that it was, and *Anna* burned down the carriage house." Erik shot him a challenging look. "She stole the comte's stallion too."

"May I know why?"

"It involved Barret's kidnapping of Christine."

"Ah. That would explain the Comte de Chagny's passion in finding you. He assumes you were involved in that? Given your penchant for kidnapping Christine?" Erik's posture told Vahid he wasn't amused. "So this goes beyond the death of Philippe de Chagny? France seems determined to bring you to justice for that."

Erik's golden eyes flared wide at the mention of that name. "I did not kill Philippe de Chagny!"

"I'm on your side, Erik!" Vahid bucked off the railing and stepped back. "I know your involvement with him. You both had me unwillingly entwined in your strange relationship from the start. You've no idea how far this has reached, do you? This goes beyond France. They've dug deep, Erik, very deep, arming themselves with whatever they can. It's more than just chandeliers and opera houses. It's your very existence. Mark my words they're obsessed with finding you. They will tear this country and any other country apart if they have to."

"They have done a lousy job thus far."

"Then why are you here?"

The remark sobered Erik instantly. Any brooding Vahid detected in him throughout the night seemed, for one second, to fall aside.

"They have Anna."

A sucking feeling compressed Vahid's stomach. That explained everything. Though he knew little about the strange relationship Erik had with this woman, he knew love in a voice when he heard it.

"I came for help, Daroga. Even a man such as I can admit to needing that. I cannot saunter to Chagny and demand they return her nor can I storm their *hôtel* here. Last I did I recall nearly getting shot." His words were as chilling as the night. "A wanted man can do little to protect his kin if he is chained. But I know they are behind this." The breeze caught Erik's cloak and fluttered it behind him. "If they have her and she breaks free, she knows where I would go. What was I to do? Stay in Germany?"

"If? You don't know they have her for certain?" Vahid felt Erik's tension as he shook his head. Vahid looked into the townhome. The music had stopped, and Simone was pouring over the maps in a large atlas, her brother acting the attentive tutor. Vahid sighed, his nerves stretched to the breaking point. "What do you plan on doing?"

Erik was overly calm as he stretched his arms wide across the balcony railing. He half looked over his shoulder back at Vahid. "I need time to think."

Vahid knew that tone. He'd heard it from Erik before in Persia; the tone of an assassin planning his next stealthy move. He didn't like it. "Think?"

"I spent all day checking the prisons, the workhouses. She is not there. They are playing games with me, Daroga. I do not like games."

No, Erik didn't. Vahid experienced that tone as well, on the back end of watching the blood Erik had spilt soak into the sand. He put as much warning as he dared into his voice.

"I'll keep Chagny's questions steered away from your whereabouts as long as I can, Erik. I suggest you keep a low profile. This is Paris after all, and you are The Phantom of the Opera. You need to be prepared for this to catch up with you."

"Let it catch up with me. I merely will not allow it to catch up with my family. Keep my children, Daroga."

Before Vahid could question him, Erik vaulted over the edge of the balcony, skimming down its walls like a spider. Vahid whipped his head back toward the house before folding himself over the railing

"Erik! You can't leave me with the children! Where are you going?"

"Where do you think, Daroga? Until I find Anna, you said it best. I am The Phantom of the Opera."

NINE

If it had helped his impatience, Vahid would have yanked the sun up the following morning with his bare hands.

Trying to explain why the best route into the opera house was via the Paris sewer system gave him a thrumming headache. Was he to saunter through the front door with two fair-skinned and phantomesque children in tow? His only option was his old tried and true route. The happy spirit of sunlight had disappeared the farther the earth swallowed them. He wasted no time that morning in following through on the decision he'd made the instant Erik left. It kept him up all night.

Keep his children! He is as mad as the day we parted in Persia. What he'd do was return his two charges to their rightful spot. With Inspector Legard breathing down his neck how was he to explain the appearance of two children in his care let alone keep them secret, especially when the little one was rather unpredictable?

I am a withering, lonely old man, you blithering idiot. Shoving your children at me is marking us all with a bulls-eye.

Moving stealthily through the abysmal corridors of Paris's darkest sewers, he grimaced every time the youth at his side cursed in German and assaulted the cobwebs. Dank passages and squealing rats seemed not to Philippe's liking. Vahid clamped his teeth.

Perhaps the lad's tastes take after his nobler namesake.

It was the little one that truly worried him. Simone seemed in her glory, tearing back her hood and gliding through the dark with what he could only describe as finesse. She poked her curly head around every corner they came by, her strange eyes blaring an intense shade of gold.

Vahid's skull split.

Out of the corner of his eyes, he saw her slide toward a shadow like liquid mercury. Lunging for her, he came up empty, but she didn't. One artful pounce had her clutching a cricket in her free hand. Shouting in delight, she shoved it toward his face.

"Ein abendlied!"

Vahid recoiled. "Pardon?"

Philippe pushed past them swatting cobwebs out of his hair. "An *abendlied*." He parroted in a mockingly immature voice.

With his patience wearing thin, Vahid rubbed his temple. "Say again?"

"Abendlied. A lullaby? An evening song?" When Vahid deepened the furrow in his brow, Philippe sighed. "Daroga, it's what she calls, oh, just listen to her cricket!"

Triumphant, Simone uncurled her fist one finger at a time to present her miniature maestro. "Well," Vahid grimaced. "That's one composer who will no longer be conducting."

Philippe took his sister's hand and flicked the smashed cricket away. He stroked her palm against his trousers, wiping off the gooey remains. "She has my father's murderous side," he rumbled.

"Lovely child."

Philippe drew Simone's hood up and pushed her on forward. "Then you're aware."

Vahid plowed past the girl, biting down hard on his loose tongue, his headache growing bigger than all the sewers combined. "I'm aware of what?"

"That my father is a murderer."

Vahid stopped dead, as did Philippe. Simone paused further

ahead, happy strings of German bubbling out her mouth as they arrived at the base of a murky underground lake. She pointed toward the water as if it were a private pond in a dark and mysterious world.

"What exactly are you asking of me?" Vahid ignored the girl and instead followed the boy's study of the eerie blue light dancing above the water.

"I'm asking for the answers my father refuses to give me about The Phantom of the Opera. No great Parisian maestro enters an opera house via a sewer unless his past is more unsavory than I suspect."

Hands on his hips, Philippe looked every bit as imposing as his father. Silent, Vahid listened.

"I know all about this blasted manhunt and how we came to be involved in it," Philippe growled in disgust, his voice echoing through the corridor. "I know my parents are innocent in the crimes that started this farce, but he murdered for a good reason. And I know my father was some—Phantom—that everyone *thinks* is mad, but any atrocities he committed were for the sake of saving Christine Daaé!"

There was not a pipe of opium long enough to ease Vahid's pounding temples.

"What I can't figure out," Philippe snapped, "is why you're taking us to him via a rat-infested sewer unless there's something more to this manhunt, and to him, to which I'm not privy."

Saved by the blonde blur out of the corner of his eyes, Vahid turned around as Simone gleefully charged toward the lake.

The water!

Moving with lightning speed, he raced forward in time to hook her into his arms before she had a chance to set foot in the frigid depths. Their bodies did an artful pirouette away from the water. He clung to her and ignored her flailing protests as he willed himself to breathe. He suspected simple country children were excellent swimmers, but not in this water, not with what mysteries he remembered it commanded. Vahid carried Simone back toward her brother and plopped her down in front of him.

"That," Vahid spat, shoving a thumb toward the lake, "is what you don't know." He pointed them in the direction of the Communard road and away, he hoped, from the past. "We'll enter this way; through the third cellar." Vahid watched with an odd sort of relief as Simone darted up the road, violin under her chin. Her lively notes lit up a place of eternal darkness.

"What don't I know? Did he kill someone else? At that lake?" Philippe's inquiry slapped Vahid in the back snapping the one nerve he had left.

If the children were his charges—then so be it. He'd do as he saw fit.

Vahid turned. He was about to enter battle worthy of heaven versus hell. There was no going back now.

"Did he kill someone else?" Vahid calmly nodded though he'd had it with the boy's questions and with Erik's messes. "Where shall we start? The assassin he was for the Sultana of Persia and all the political murders he committed? With a fallen chandelier and the poor concierge that died beneath it, or perhaps with Philippe Georges Marie, the Comte de Chagny? Did he drown him or not? Maybe he tried to—on the first attempt!"

The silence that followed was a blissful tonic to Vahid's pounding head.

Twisting the children more times than a rat in a maze, Vahid breathed apprehensively in relief as they emerged from shadow into Erik's inner sanctum. Philippe hadn't said a word since Vahid likely ruined his life. He'd have to set aside his remorse and focus on what would happen next. Erik would probably snap his neck that much was certain. The stench of mildew and neglect met his nose and made it crease. Remnants of Erik's unpredictable wrath lay strewed around the room. It was not the unusual house Vahid remembered of years ago, but it still held the same sense of blood-chilling stillness. It whipped up his instinct to protect, causing him to grab for Simone's shoulders. Vahid held her back as Philippe cautiously stepped forward. Whatever conflicting emotions surged in the boy's head after what Vahid told him was anyone's guess, but the sheer magnitude of his expression bespoke of a rising storm.

"Where are we?" Philippe harshly whispered. "Where's my father?"

Vahid kept his focus on Simone. Being back down in Erik's lair made trepidation crawl up his spine like a resurrected long-dead spider. It settled on the back of his neck where it kept twitching. The monster could be anywhere in the uncharted bowels of the theater. He pressed Simone close against his legs. She did all she could to pop out of his grip.

"Is this some sort of jest? You don't mean to tell me my father *lived* here?"

Vahid remained stoic and watched the boy's jaw move as he ground his teeth. Philippe made a circumspect inspection of his father's past. The youth wandered amongst broken furniture and peered around corners into other rooms. His posture was tense when he left the Louis-Philippe room; his eyes downcast. When he spied the pedal board of the organ, his tension evaporated, and the boy appeared to flare to life. Vahid tried not to react when Philippe whipped his head back to him as if searching for answers. The boy crept toward the instrument as if it would burst into life at any moment. The room beyond, however, stopped him in his tracks. Philippe shoved his arm backward and pointed.

"What kind of perverse joke is this, Daroga? Why is a coffin down here?"

"Come away from there, Philippe."

The voice, gentle as a bleating lamb but as forceful as a hurricane, swirled around the room. Philippe turned just as Erik emerged from a shadow. He took form from the darkness, a parchment in one hand, his other, reaching toward Simone. Small flicks of his bony fingers beckoned his daughter to him. Vahid held fast as soon as he felt the little girl squirm to get away.

"I'm not letting go of her until I know you're in command of all your senses, Erik. When you need time to think the outcome is usually disastrous."

The reply didn't rise in pitch but instead poured out with deadly intensity. "There is only one sense I am barely in command of now, Daroga, and that is my anger. How dare you bring my children here?"

"With Chagny lurking they can't stay with me. I would have explained that last night if you hadn't disappeared like a Phantom."

"So you bring them *here*? Even I had the presence of mind not to!"

"Why not?" Philippe's outburst sliced the room in two like a guillotine. "If this place is your past, Father, then this ours as well, regardless of what you try to keep from us. Mainly a certain Philippe Georges Marie, the Comte de Chagny! What else have you neglected to tell me?"

Vahid gripped the child in front of him as Erik lunged forward. That name triggered a tension so palpable he could have ripped it off the air. The monster leaned into his son.

"How do you know of him?"

Vahid stiffened. A paralyzing foreboding flowed through Vahid's veins as he waited for a fraction of a second it took for the monster to explode.

"Him?" Erik pointed to Vahid. "You are to believe nothing that great twit tells you! Nothing, Erik says! It is your mother who speaks the truth of our past and how *dare* you believe the words of anyone over her!"

Vahid felt a bead of sweat trickled down his neck. He held on to Simone tighter.

"Mother's story only collaborated yours," Philippe shouted back. "But it makes too much sense now, doesn't it? The reason why Chagny pursues us so relentlessly isn't that of some murder in self-defense to help a nobleman's wife, and some misconstrued story about opera houses and con men, but things beyond this manhunt—*far beyond*! You *are* mad, aren't you?"

"I am not a madman!"

A low rumble came from Erik as he shoved past his son. Up and down he paced as if to smother a volcano erupting inside of him. Vahid watched the same tension start to shake Philippe. He swore the boy was going to punch something. It was as if Vahid looked into a strange mirror that reflected only personalities.

Philippe, seemingly knowing that he was weaker in comparison to his father, eventually looked to his side in defeat.

Vahid clenched his jaw. *That boy loves you Erik—mad or not. He only wants to understand.* Vahid let go of Simone long enough to gesture one-handed for Philippe to come to him. It was enough of an opening for the girl to break free and race toward her father. Erik grabbed for his daughter and scooped her up into his long arms in one deft motion. He perched her on one hip.

"Believe what you wish of me, Philippe, but keep your head about you, lest the sins of the father become the sins of the son. We are not mad."

"Then prove it. Let me help." Philippe's voice was a thin and passionate whisper.

Bold words for such youth. "I can only do so much for you, Erik, but don't involve the boy in this. I implore you." Vahid chose his words with caution, ceasing to breathe as Erik raised his hands to his mask.

The monster lowered it and tossed it to a table. Vahid hitched his breath and felt the pressure grip his chest. It had been years since he had seen the supreme ugliness of the Opera Ghost unmasked. Erik lowered Simone to the ground and dropped the hood of her cloak to her shoulders. Kneeling, he tenderly drew his hand down her bony cheek. This time a mirror of a different sort was present, and Vahid couldn't help but stare aghast at father and daughter. They were mirror images of each other; the curse on their faces equally repulsive, yet somehow, seeing their supreme deformities side-by-side made the horror easier to look upon.

"No more hiding this face," Erik said numbly. "She will never be made to suffer as I have."

"*Was ist los?*" Simone said, cocking her head. She glanced over her shoulder toward her brother. It broke Vahid's heart to see her gleaming tears. "Philippe? *Was ist los?*"

"What is wrong? Everything and nothing, Simone," Philippe replied. His voice had cracked.

The monster came toward them, his strange eyes filled with an intensity making Vahid wonder if he was capable of reading souls. He held out the parchment he still clutched in his hand. Neatly folded and franked with a macabre seal, Vahid's eyes slapped on the name Erik had written on the front. There were limits to what he was willing to do in servitude to the Phantom.

"Not again, Erik. Don't start in with your infernal notes."

Philippe snatched it instead, making Vahid curse. The boy asked no questions and made no other comments instead he lowered the brief to his side and stared at Erik with all the seriousness of a time-hardened man. One way or another Philippe was determined to gain access to his father even if being his advocate was the way to do so. The boy had no idea what he was getting himself into.

"Don't let him do this, Erik. I'm warning you; this is not the way."

"As if your warnings have any impact on me." Erik turned to his son. "Leave with the Persian. Have him escort you to the post and see to it that is mailed," he instructed. "If I cannot go to the comte, he can come to me. I am certain he will seek me out once he reads that. The noble fool is predictable."

There was not a single sweet cloud of smoke that could numb the alliance Vahid watched form. Philippe merely wanted his mother back and Erik, his family intact. What right had he to judge? Were they all not servants of the truth and the truth often attended by danger? A light came back into Philippe. A light Vahid didn't like.

As if Erik read his mind, he spoke. "Daroga, I have behaved long enough."

The melancholy playing of a violin tripped Vahid's thoughts away from speaking up. Distilled in those achingly confused notes were the reasons he kept his silence and slowly allowed himself to be written into the Phantom's opera again. He slipped the note from Philippe's hand without a further word.

Through the violin, a little girl wept tears only a mother could soothe.

TEN

Headaches put Raoul in a foul mood, especially when they assaulted him first thing in the morning and lasted well throughout the day. The aroma of aged oak stung his nostrils as he poured two fingers of cognac. Maybe the drink would dull his pounding head. What didn't dull, was the knocking on his library door.

What now? "Enter!"

As if he needed interruptions? Christine's displeasure over Anna Barret had rattled his brain enough. He experienced the brunt of her seething anger all day yesterday, listening to it with half an ear. Even André wasn't happy with him, and Raoul couldn't blame his son. To have been out on the town with Christine while she was in a mood could be like riding next to an ice-cube. Her cold silence could freeze hell. Raoul shook his head and stared into his drink before setting the glass down. He should be thanking the stars his son was willing to take her out again. When his wife wished it, she could hit notes in her frustration that could shatter eardrums. Whoever was about to disturb his peace today would get the brunt of his ill humor. Raoul presented the footman bowing respectfully in the doorway with his best nailing look after the man announced his uninvited visitor. He slammed the crystal cap back on the decanter.

"Let him in," Raoul snapped. The Persian was not exactly a sight for sore eyes as he strode into the room, a bit too casually for Raoul's temperament. "Daroga, to what do I owe the pleasure? Are you here with news or merely seeking a libation away from the scrutiny of critics?" He scooped up his glass again, tossed back the drink, winced, and thumped his snifter down. "Actually, Daroga, ignore that inquiry and just tell me why you're here."

"I always did enjoy the Chagny civility," the Persian replied drolly.

Raoul stroked a thumb across his lips. It was a means to block what he really wanted to say about this impromptu meeting. He had a fugitive sequestered in his servant's quarters and a less than sane bounty hunter stinking up his halls. He moved his hand, punching the words away in a silent command for his guest to keep talking.

"Before I begin, may I ask where your wife is?" the dark man inquired.

The brow Raoul hitched lifted a notch higher than his patience. "She is out for the day, so if you wish to speak with her, leave your card. I have a matter at hand to which I don't want her subjected."

"I should say you do." The Persian slid a note toward him. "I've little idea where that came from or who delivered it, but that seal and red-ink are unmistakable. It appeared on my desk when I woke this morning. Beyond this, I have nothing additional for you."

The Persian kept blinking. Why couldn't he keep his focus? He was hiding something, perhaps even lying. It burned Raoul more than the cognac and oddly written note. Its sloppy strokes, as if the author never learned to join his letters, studied him like the jaws of a serpent poised to strike. Unfolding it, he read aloud.

Fondest greetings Monsieur le Comte:

My sincerest regards. I hope the years have brought you the best comfort, however; that

being said, the pleasantries of this note end here. Your endless pursuit of me has drawn to a close. I request your audience, and I highly suggest you show up. I will be frightfully blunt for I find it rather suits me, and though I am an enemy of scandal, there is no avoiding what is about to befall you. You should know by now it is best not to raise my temper.

Raoul's gaze tightened as he looked from the note to its messenger.

It is for the sake of the innocent that I barely keep my temper in check. If you ever wished to know how to anger me, you have found out.

Heed my warning: Proceed with caution Monsieur; you have toyed with my heirs.

Ph. of the O.

It took a few seconds to register the signature, the scarlet ink, the matchstick-like scrawl and the tone of the note. The icy wave that jerked Raoul's spine sobered him the instant his glare punched the Persian in the face.

"Where is he? At the Garnier?"

"I took the liberty to search the Garnier already. It is as you left it years ago."

"Did you now? How fortuitous of you. Perhaps instead you've been lying and covering for him." He slapped the letter down on the blotter. "This simply 'appeared' on your desk? Do you take me for a fool? Where is he?" A lack of patience made the muscles around his right eye jump.

"Moreover than that, where is Mademoiselle Barret?" The Persian parried in a tone only a former investigator could summon. "He cares little over where your wife is apparently. You should worry about her and take care to keep the two women separate."

As if Raoul didn't know that and had not spent the morning flaying himself for permitting Anna to sit like a target in his house. "Why come here and advise me of this if you don't have any information?" The adrenaline filling him took excellent care of curbing his rising headache.

"I'm only doing as you wish of me, Monsieur."

"Mademoiselle Barret is here." Raoul ground his teeth together as if chewing back his words. The Persian scrutinized him. There was something behind his eyes, like a spark of recognition. The man would be a horrible poker player.

"Keeping Mademoiselle Barret here is fodder for *L'Epoch* if word ever gets out," the Persian said. "How did you come by her?"

"I'm well aware of *L'Epoch*." Raoul reached for the cognac again having a hard time keeping the sarcasm from rolling off his tongue. "I sent Loup to Germany a while back with instructions to uncover whatever he could. I wasn't expecting Anna Barret to arrive on my doorstep. Her maddening silence, not to mention my wife's screeching, could make me a drunkard if I didn't find such despicable." He gestured with the drink. "You can blame my demandable conscious for her tenure here. Regardless of her crimes, I can't see a woman in prison, at least not on my head. She looks like she's been through enough. Once in Brussels it will be out of my hands." The girl's bruising came to mind with his next sip.

"You intend to send Mademoiselle Barret to Belgium?"

"Such is the only solution at this point. I will make the arrangements this afternoon. I can't keep her here until she confesses what she knows—*L'Epoch* you know. " Raoul smiled cynically. "Let the Brussels authorities close of this one unsavory chapter in my life. My huntsman can deal with her from now on." Warming his drink with his palm, Raoul shook his head. The insufferable intolerance he had for his bounty hunter gnawed at him through the years. Loup had been a necessary and often uncontrollable evil.

"From what I know of him his methods are unorthodox and often immoral. Are you mad? Release her into my custody.

Perhaps I can get her to talk."

Raoul lowered his glass. The cognac did little but rot him inside out anyway. "Truly? What cares have you if she's here or in Brussels for justice? Unless you know where Erik is, and your passion is a result of some misplaced loyalty to him and the girl?"

"I have interrogated men for far more years than any of you combined. She won't speak to you because you're the enemy, Monsieur."

Raoul lifted the note and tapped it on the desk before gesturing to the door with it. "We shall see about that. I have the upper hand now. Perhaps this note and a shock to her system will make her talk."

→»•••————•••————•••«←

Anna tripped over the length of her skirts as Loup hauled her through the halls. Flanked on her other side by Legard, she forced herself to stare forward. She was getting dizzy volleying her head between the two. They came for her out of nowhere, abruptly plucking her from a dark room in the root cellar to hasten through the maze of the massive townhome. They ended within the comte's private library. He stood center of the ornate room, his expression less than pleasant. To his side was a man she hadn't seen in years, but whose eyes were as unmistakable as Erik's.

The Persian!

Anna forced her attention away from him lest the recognition flicker in her eyes.

"Am I to assume you still have nothing to say?" The comte strode forward.

Looking from him to the Persian, she caught the slight flare to his nostrils that bid her hold her tongue.

"I told you all I know, Monsieur," she replied curiously.

He extended a note. "Go on. Read it. Your friend over here," he gestured to the Persian, "delivered it. I suspect you two know each other?"

Anna stared at the page. It took all her might not to yank her study away from those scarlet letters and look toward the center of Paris. She shook her head denying she knew the dark man and prayed the lie didn't dance openly in her posture.

"You've lied to me, Mademoiselle," the comte said.

Anna's neck cramped. She let the page fall to her side and replied with a careless shrug. "I've no idea who your strange looking friend is, and I told you already. I've not seen Erik in years." The note crunched as she shoved it back into his hands. "And what makes you think I can read?"

Inside her belly churned. She *could* read, and Erik was angry—violently so. But he was here! Why had he sought the Persian? Were they to be allies? Did he know where Erik was? Certain Erik's madness was on the rise; the desperation to make it to his side threatened to make her explode.

"Nothing you say matters any longer, Mademoiselle. Since you've been uncooperative, you're heading to Belgium where you will meet justice for the crimes you've committed there. All I need to know is in that letter anyway."

"Belgium?" She prayed the Persian would read her panic.

"Scaring the accused rarely works, Monsieur le Comte. I think you are better off keeping the Mademoiselle here."

Anna bit her tongue. The Persian had annunciated the last word. Erik *was* in Paris!

Anna played off the Persian's lead. "I've no business in Belgium any more than I do here."

"I judge by the past, Mademoiselle, which is the only definition by which man should be judged. Once in Belgium, the authorities will take it from there. That is unless you have certain information that may help me settle my affairs here?"

Anna thought she registered a twitch to his upper lip that made his fine blonde mustache jump. Nerves? She made sure to keep her expression neutral.

"I told you all I know."

She bit her cheek until she could bear the pain of it no longer. Anna had mad a horrible mistake with her outburst to the comtesse. If she relayed the information of her children with Erik to the comte, there was no telling what would happen. She had to get out of there.

"I suspect this entire thing is a ploy on your behalf to get me to speak," she said, trying to appear unfazed. "Anyone can pen a note to you and claim it to be from the Phantom. I'm afraid you've built quite the reputation."

The comte jerked his head over his shoulder, indicating door. "Legard, take her. Ready a carriage for Belgium."

"Monsieur le Comte," The Persian bid as Legard and Loup sandwiched her in-between them. "You're going about this the wrong way. You must appeal to a woman's natural instinct."

The comte rolled air over his tongue. "What would *that* be, Daroga?"

"She claims she can't read and I believe her. So we inform her that the note mentions heirs. Have you any children, Mademoiselle?"

The Persian had weighed her down with a heavy look. Anna search around her as if perplexed by it all.

"You need not answer." He turned to the comte. "Give her time alone to reflect on that implication and perhaps she will spill all. You have to toy with a woman's motherly nature. There's no telling what could happen to orphaned children, after all."

Anna caught the nearly imperceptible nod of his head. He was trying to keep her from Brussels! Biding time! Anna licked her lips. Look nervous. Act like he'd hit a nerve. The comte smirked. Anna stifled a sigh of relief… it was working.

"It is either you think on that, and what could happen to your family or you return to Brussels," the Persian warned.

Anna opened her mouth to speak but was cut short.

"Will you all learn how to handle a woman and be done with this? Beat it out of her!" Loup's left hand cut through the air sideways and contacted with stinging force against her temple, knocking her into Legard.

Before she could even cry from the pain, or acknowledge the resulting shout of protests from Legard and the Persian, the comte rounded. Like a rock from a catapult, his fist smashed the side of Loup's jaw flattening the bounty hunter to the floor. Reaching down, he grabbed him by the collar and brought their faces inches apart.

"I'll not have any woman abused as a result of this! Get yourself under control in regards to her or I swear you'll not walk away from his manhunt intact."

Loup writhed on the ground, purple with fury as the comte shoved him backward and stepped off. Anna backed away, her hand against her throbbing head. She searched the Persian's eyes for what to expect next.

"Monsieur le Comte, though you act in all good honor, you're a complete and utter fool!" The Persian stood boldly at Anna's side. He locked a hand around her upper arm. She gasped and looked from him to the comte, to Legard, and finally down to Loup's billowing rage.

"Angering a man like Loup then sending her off with him will only kill her!" The Persian pointed out. Anna felt a slight pressure to her upper arm as if signaling to her that he was using the situation to her advantage. "Didn't you just regret the abuse she's already endured?"

Anna's eyes flew open in shock. The comte had sympathy toward her?

"Regret?" Loup growled, bolting to his feet. He lunged toward the comte, his voice thundering like an angry stallion let loose. "*Regret*? You miserable dog! You dare *regret* how I manage this manhunt? No one regrets my services! I'm the best bloody huntsman in Europe!" Loup rounded on Anna, grabbing her opposite arm and hauling her out of The Persian's grip.

"What do you think you are doing?" The comte moved swiftly, blocking Loup's path.

"Taking what is mine. I've waited long enough for Anna Barret. She's mine anyway. That is what we agreed upon at the start of this manhunt. I'm not about to let you keep her here while you dance around tracking down your Phantom. Any idiot would just go to the opera house, put a bullet in his head and be done with it by now."

"We don't know for certain he is there," Raoul shouted. "Mademoiselle Barret—"

"Could be your perfect bargaining chip if you had a single ounce of man in you!" Loup snarled. He pointed an imaginary gun to Anna's temple. "You want your little ghost; you merely reply to his note and tell him you have his whore at the end of steel and see how fast he comes running. Or perchance you are too afraid that your wife will go running *toward* him and not *away* from him?"

"Enough! Restrain him!"

The comte's sharp command shattered the air around them. In the blink of an eye, Legard was on Loup, pinning his arms behind his back. The sudden move tumbled Anna to the side and into the Persian. His whisper was as soft and fleeting.

"Keep your mouth shut on what you know, but play the worried mother—anything to keep the comte from sending you off. He's sympathetic toward women. I think he'll hold you here. I'll inform Erik and your children, you're safe and will stall Chagny all I can. Monsieur le Comte," he called out. "What is your intention? Anger that huntsman further?"

"Get him out of here," Raoul growled to Legard. "I'm done with him. His tenure here is over. Mademoiselle Barret will remain in Chagny custody until she tells me what I want to know—for the sake of her children."

The Persian slightly shook her arm to prove his plan was in motion.

"You deny me Anna? Deny me what is mine?" Loup bucked, shouting at the comte as Legard hauled him toward the doors. "Burn in hell, you shit! I play by my rules and will have what is mine!" Sharply butting Legard aside with his shoulder he freed himself from his grip and tapped his temple with that imaginary pistol. "This is far from over now."

Anna leaned into the Persian's grip attempting to back away from Loup as he propelled himself toward the streets of Paris, cursing all the way.

ELEVEN

"I am beginning to understand why you avoid this place, *Maman*."

Thumbing his watch back in his pocket for the third time, André unenthusiastically eyed the filling theater. In the past, the opera rejuvenated him despite the mysterious stigma of the Phantom lurking around his parents. Now, knowing all the facts and how they tied in with his beloved uncle, the Chagny box at the Garnier was suffocating.

"André, I'm not happy in the least of your father's decisions to keep that woman around, but what is done is done." His mother laid a hand on his arm, preventing him from removing his watch again. "If I could have kept this all from you forever I would have. I don't like Mademoiselle Barret being under our noses either, but we must respect how your father handles this. Once done, let's hope the opera will bring happy memories."

André stared down at the curtain as they waited for the second act. To his side, his mother waved graciously at the patrons acknowledging her from below. Once a diva, always a diva. The Garnier soaked up every bit of her fame whenever she'd make an appearance. André wondered what fame was more alluring, the fame from her life as an opera protégé or the notoriety from being the Phantom's fantasy.

Taking his mother out on the town had done little to calm her jitters yesterday and did little to ease his today. She seemed distracted the entire coach ride. He drove with her along the Seine watching the morning sun wane to afternoon, pampered her over lunch, purchased her a new pearl necklace and ended with an evening carriage ride through the Boise, all along listening to her claim how like his father he was.

Highly unlikely. He would have ended this farce years ago by killing the Phantom the instant opportunity arose. The notes of musicians warming up swirled around them like disorganized bees. Glancing to his mother, he noted the pinch to her brow. Her unusual calm was another well-performed stage trick. She wasn't as comfortable in the opera house any longer as she'd like the world to think. Unlike her, he wasn't an actor and couldn't bear to sit in the theater one minute longer.

"I'll return. I need a bit of air before act two."

As soon as the door to the box closed behind him he shot his breath out his mouth. Never had this lifelong manhunt affected him so much. He needed to walk off his anxiety before stress aged him so much no young lady would ever pass an eye to him.

And there were plenty of young ladies to choose from at a performance like this. The opera house was the epicenter of the arts for Paris, and the halls were brimming with theatergoers. Meyerbeer drew large crowds capable of creating frenzy, yet for Philippe, a frenzy of a different sort was buzzing his head. His father was going to kill him.

"Simone?" he rumbled.

If he was able to find his sister in catacombs beneath the monastery back home, why couldn't he find her in an opera house? Charged with one task of minding her while his father up and disappeared—again—and she was gone in the blink of an eye. His nostrils flared.

So I take my eyes off her to thumb through an abandoned score of my father's. Does that warrant this death sentence?

Philippe kept his head down as he wove his way through the corridors and tried not to look conspicuous. Not easy to do when weaving the wrong way through crowds of silk and satin. He bit back a curse. He was in the most fantastic building he'd ever seen; a place where he could practically taste music, and his panic was leaving a sour flavor in his mouth. At some point in his wandering, he'd made a very wrong turn, exiting the back hallways and entering the vestibule. Philippe blamed his father for not giving him some form of orientation to the theater, and for holding him hostage in the cellars. His father did little but pace in those infernal vaults beneath the theater. The daroga was no help. He'd escorted Philippe as far as the post that morning, only to decide not to permit him to mail the letter. Philippe could do nothing but swallow his pride as the daroga marched him right back to the opera house. He was deposited back at the disgusting sewers they initially entered and left behind like a broken, useless wheel. Philippe punched his thigh in frustration.

I should have delivered that letter! I'm not some incapable child! When will they all understand that?

But here he was instead playing keeper to Simone's unpredictability. Though Philippe was unwilling to enter the depths of the theater when the Persian left him, he did so anyway. He could have followed the daroga. It took everything he had to press forward and retrace his way to his father's—what was that place anyway? Home? Labyrinth? Hell, that is what it was. A rotted, damp, hell. He did so only for Simone's sake. Not that he had to. She had spent the last several hours until their father took off again, following him stride-for-stride as he paced. To her, that abysmal lair was the greatest thing next to *linzertorte*. Philippe shoved a hand through his hair. He wanted to go home. The longer he missed his mother, the angrier he became. The more he thought on the bizarre transformation of his father the more confused Philippe became. Having Simone disappear was the last thing he needed.

It's not my fault if my sister tends to unhinge lately. "Simone!" he called again.

Philippe attempted to keep to corners and shadows, though he felt like the limelight was flaring at his feet. He couldn't be more terribly out of place. The theater was in full swing for the evening with well-dressed people roaming everywhere. Wherever everywhere was. He was utterly lost. Philippe had been covering the grounds of the opera house for hours; the halls, the streets outside, looking for his sister.

Not wanting to stand out in his simpler country garb, he picked up his pace and rounded a corner full-stride. "Simone, I swear when I get my hands on you I'm going to—*Gott!*"

"*Dieu!*"

The collision slammed him and his additional expletives, flat on his back. Air burst out his lungs with a hot, strangled moan as Philippe stared star-struck at a giant chandelier. He had no idea if he'd hit a marble column, a mirror, or a person. It took a few seconds for him to work off the crushing pain that wrapped around his chest until he got air back in his lungs. Shaking his head clear, Philippe realized it wasn't any column he hit. A hand shot down to him.

"I beg your pardon, Monsieur. I should have been paying mind to what was in front of me and not the time."

Looking beyond an elaborate signet ring and up the forearm of the finest eveningwear he ever saw, Philippe clapped eyes with a youth his age.

"Pay it no mind," he muttered, clasping the forearm and rising. He leaned his hands on his knees for a second before straightening.

"You're not injured?" the stranger asked. Fuzzy headed, Philippe shook his head. "Well, thank *Dieu* for that. I assume it takes more than a crash to marble to hurt one of the Garnier's stagehands, but what are you doing out here?"

Stagehand? Philippe scowled and brushed his trousers, which was a useless gesture since the floors were so clean a surgeon would be at home. "I'm not a stagehand, Monsieur."

"My pardon. I just assumed by your attire."

Of course, he did. Philippe offered a tight smile. An elephant might as well have been roaming the halls, and he still would have looked out of place. The young man before him looked fancier than the rest of the patrons around him, and his tone insisted Philippe answer. He scrubbed the back of his neck and concocted the best lie he could. "Ah, my sister darted in here to get out of the rain. I appear to have lost her. I beseech you not to call the authorities. I'll be on my way as soon as I locate her."

"Why would I do that? Every man has a right to duck out of this abysmal Paris weather. Come," he pointed down a corridor. "We'll let the management know, and every available hand will search for her."

"That's really not—"

"No arguments. Her age?" They began to walk.

"Seven."

"A child! Too young to be on her own. We'll pick up our pace." He extended his hand as they walked. "Perhaps this is a bit forward of our acquaintance so soon, but I'm nothing if not unconventional, you may call me André."

Philippe stared at the gesture before accepting it and shaking his hand. "Philippe. My sister is Simone."

"I detect an accent to your French. German is it?"

Philippe nodded being put at ease by André's friendly presence. "This is my first time in Paris. My sister gets a bit overly excited, I'm afraid."

"First time? You don't say? My mother is a Prima Donna, she studied and sang here."

Philippe tripped over his feet and nearly met the floor again. A prima donna. Jealousy chewed at his gut; what he wouldn't give to have grown up in and around music.

André casually tugged on the sleeves of his waistcoat and turned them down another corridor. "This opera house has been a part of my family for generations."

Philippe bit his tongue. When had he ever been jealous; being raised around monks it was hardly an emotion he explored. He was tempted to best André by blurting out that his maestro of a father had much to do with the facility also.

"Is your father a stagehand here as well? Came for work, did you?" André questioned cheerfully.

Small talk was not exactly what Philippe desired right now, and frankly, the answer to that question was a clear-cut no. "My father is a carpenter," he rumbled, almost impossible to keep the disdain of that sentence off his tongue.

As if on cue, Philippe's words served as a divide between their classes. André went silent. Wandering down the marbled hall unsettled Philippe as much as it excited him. Eyeing themselves as they passed by floor to ceiling mirrors, they were a complete contradiction; André the picture of wealth and class, Philippe the picture of—what? He refused to look in a mirror to find out. In Germany, he knew who he was. The son of Erik who lived at the monastery and who delighted in doing anything he could for the benefit of the monks, with an occasional excursion to do anything he could for the *fräuleins* of the village. The music in him was a sleeping mystery. Here, it cracked open like a roaring monster. The opera house was the most fantastic place he'd ever been, and the one man who could lay a world of music at his feet was ensconced in its bowels like some perverse nightmare. The vestibule they were in opened to an opulent entry and Philippe found he stared in wonder at the Grand Escalier.

Drawn to the details like a bee to honey, he couldn't help but rotate in his spot—how he longed to run his hand along the detailed columns. With a curious smile, he studied the scantily clad female sculptures that held the gaslights aloft. He approached the three staircases when his daydream came to a crashing halt.

"This way, Monsieur. Patrons only up those stairs." André pointed down an empty hall.

Philippe swallowed his disappointment, which ended in a choking cough as soon as he heard and the all-to-familiar strings of a violin.

"Blast," he whispered, checking his guide. André heard the music too, and before it grew any louder, Philippe spun around one of the risqué lamps and dashed in its direction down the lower staircases.

He found Simone staring intently into a dark alcove beneath the lower ramps of the Escalier. Hood off, her head was cocked curiously. She gazed at the statue of a woman with her arms outstretched as if she were reaching for some unknown thought or sound. Lightly tripping tones undulated off Simone's violin. Philippe looked around him. Luckily most patrons were upstairs, yet if Simone kept playing, she'd send crowds rushing to her in no time at all. Upon seeing her brother, she pointed with her bow, momentarily silencing the instrument.

"Does she hear birds in her head too?"

Philippe looked over his shoulder to see André jogging down the stairs. Yanking Simone's hood up, he smothered her face into his hip.

"You've found her I take it?" André chirped.

"Yes, thank you kindly for your assistance, Monsieur—"

Simone's tiny fist pummeled Philippe's legs as her violin batted him on the rump. He shrugged at André scowl.

"Sisters," Philippe laughed as he muffled her cries best he could. "You know how they are—ow!"

Stomping hard on his foot, Simone wiggled his grip and shot a look to André. Philippe's heart stilled as she blurted the query to him.

"Does she hear birds in her head or not?"

Startled André laughed at Philippe. "Seems I've found the perfect opportunity to brush up on my German." He crouched to Simone's level and replied in her native tongue. "Now why would she hear birds in her head?"

Philippe held his breath. Simone's expression lit up likely happy she could speak to someone besides him and their father. Everything in his gut said this was about to go from bad to worse. Stripping her hood off, Simone eagerly replied.

"Because she looks happy, which means she would sound peach like your voice does and your voice looks *very* peach. What are you happy about?"

"For the love of God!" André cried, losing his balance and stumbling backward.

Philippe sucked in his breath as the back of André's hand shot to cover his mouth. The alcove they stood in was just dark enough that her piercing yellow eyes shone in the shadows.

Simone stepped closer to André, causing his eyes to widen even more. She swatted at the air in front of him. "Oh no. Too much black fog now. What's the matter? Are you afraid of birds?"

"*Nein!*" he stammered, scrambling to his feet.

"Then what is it? You look like you're going to be sick. They're only birds."

"What in the name of Christ is wrong with her?" André shouted in French, as he backed away.

Simone tucked her violin under her arm and looked aghast at her brother then back to André. Her confusion shattered Philippe's heart.

"Silence your tongue now," Philippe hissed back at him, his French feeling hot out his mouth, "and speak of us to no-one. She's merely a little girl!"

Gathering Simone into his arms, he yanked her hood up and shoved beyond his startled guide. Philippe hastened down the closest corridor he could find.

"Wait," André called out behind him. "Your forgiveness, please! My shock was only natural."

Philippe cursed under his breath and quickened his stride. Blast the prejudicial world! Judgment was *not* natural. Setting his jaw he stopped when a hand on his shoulder prevented his escape. With great pressure growing in his chest, he turned.

"Your forgiveness, please." André reached into his jacket pocket and extended a card. "Allow me to make it up to you at some—" he looked at Simone, "—less pressing time."

Philippe snatched the card and crammed it in his pocket not bothering to read the name. Turning, he continued into shadows. "Some other time, perhaps."

"Might I know who may call on me, Monsieur? Your full name?"

Philippe stopped again and met Simone's perplexed look. They didn't have surnames. That jealousy twisted in him again. What would he place on a calling card: Son of Erik? Glancing over his shoulder to André, he offered all he could before hastening to any sanctuary he could find.

"Philippe Georges Marie."

Fist to his mouth Philippe crouched with his back against a marble column. Listening to Simone's wavering notes, he wondered if it were blessing or sickness that plagued his sister. On and on she bowed, her notes vibrating from one side of the hall to the next. They wove unseen webs capable of entrapping any who dared to wander too close. If he closed his eyes, her music carried him through that web, away to levels of himself he didn't know existed. Philippe wasn't sure of anything in his life beyond wanting to discover that plane of reality within him. Staring blankly at the floor, he watched Simone's reflection move as she moved. Secluded enough in some random hall, no one seemed to hear her music, and for that he was thankful. Philippe didn't know how to return to his father's labyrinth, and he didn't want to. What would he say to him when he did? That the last several hours of trying to track down his sister while his father was off hiding had worsened his need for answers? That the boy he'd met was the enemy? His ragging breathing moistened the card he clutched in his fist.

Simone's music changed to short, cautious notes, like a butterfly tripping over an unpredictable breeze. Concerned, he glanced down the hall to find her staring intently at her reflection in an ornate mirror. Rising, his legs went numb. Angry, wild notes poured out of her violin next, as if that butterfly banged against a chrysalis with no means of escape. Simone had not often seen her reflection and judging from her music this time; she was confused by what she saw.

That arrogant nobleman and his accursed reaction! The card crushed in his hand. *André Thaddeus Marie, Vicomte de Changy, Faubourg St. Germain, Paris.* Why wasn't Philippe surprised to know the identity of that boy. It was always Chagny that shifted and changed his life, just like it changed Simone's music.

Unable to bear the way she stood motionless as she played, he hastened to her. Gently, he turned her away from what she saw. The music she played spoke what his soul could not, and he desperately needed her to be that extension of him. Dropping to one knee, he brushed the air on either side of her as if wiping away any invisible hurts that might change her music.

"None will look at you like that again. I swear on my life. None will look on you that way again."

As if his words were a balm to an innocent soul, her foot began to tap, her hips swayed, and she played on, this time spinning around him like a thousand tops, carefree and happy. Philippe vowed to see to it her music always sounded that way, and it would start by avenging his mother and making demands of Chagny.

He didn't know his way back to the labyrinth, but he could find the *Faubourg St. Germain.*

TWELVE

With André gone, Christine was able to let the full weight of the opera house dropped around her like a leaded cloak. Act two began, but Christine gave no care to any of it. Tears leaked out as memories connecting her to the theater ran like a river through her.

Anna Barret was in custody, but where was Erik? Raoul would be furious at her and André for coming to the theater in light of the developments. But as much as the opera house made her shoulders droop, it was also the only place she felt at home. Christine rolled a shoulder trying to shrug off her heavy thoughts. One weighty thought she couldn't remove was that Erik would not be happy about the capture of Anna Barret. It was only a matter of time before he showed up. Just the idea of Erik rushing to Paris in search of that woman made Christine's chest tight. She didn't accept for one minute that Anna didn't know Erik's whereabouts and she refused to believe anything about them having children.

What a tangled, insurmountable mess. Christine wished to hang Anna with her lies, but in the next second, she wanted to go on living in denial. She discretely rubbed her temple with the tip of a finger, as she let the entire mess sink in. Being at the opera always drew attention her way, she didn't want anyone to know how much being there made her heart ache.

She couldn't let Erik be arrested and carted off to death. But if she didn't, what will everyone suspect? If Christine interfered with Erik's capture in any way her family name may be scandalized, and she'd already done enough to place it in jeopardy.

Christine leaned her head against her hand. It all seemed highly impossible she would ever find a way out of her ruin.

The door opened. For a second Christine's breath hitched as she looked toward Box Five. If she were hoping to see Erik, she would be disappointed. Christine let out her breath as André sat next to her. One look at him and an unshakeable sense of apprehension tightened her shoulders. Never had she seen her son so pale. Christine laid a hand on his forearm.

"André, what is it?"

With a finger perched across his upper lip and his elbow digging into the velvet arm of the chair he looked at her before staring emptily out across the theater. "What did the Phantom look like?"

Gooseflesh instantly pebbled her skin, and she fought not to glance back toward Box Five again. She stammered silently as André's hand crushed harder against his mouth.

It took him a while to find words to continue. "I just encountered something I wish to heaven I could tear from my eyes, for never in my life have I ever witnessed such supreme horror on any living soul."

Christine's heart lurched while at the same time shook with anticipation none would understand.

"There is a face to Death, with yellow eyes in this opera house," he whispered.

Christine bit her inner lip. His next question twisted her spleen until she feared all the blood drained from her body.

"What did the Phantom look like, *Maman*?"

She stared at him with a shocked blankness only reserved for those unaware of their senses. She spoke slowly and looked over his shoulder, off to the distance in her mind. "Once you've seen his face, it burns your mind and nothing can eliminate what it tattoos upon your soul." The once-warm pearls around her neck now felt bitterly cold. "You've seen this? He's here?"

"No."

Jerking her hand off his arm as if it were suddenly on fire, Christine's heart plummeted to the floor. Was she relieved or devastated? She cornered her son when their eyes met.

"André. What do you mean?" Her face contorted begging him to relieve her of this torture. "What have you seen?"

"What righteous God curses a little girl in such a manner and gives her flawless brother my *uncle's* name?"

Somewhere in the madness of her son's words, Christine felt Erik's presence in all his strength and glory—just as she had in the past. She leaned away from André, painfully conscious of how much he reflected his father. His tone had the same determination for answers as Raoul's did years ago when this manhunt began. The emotion was clogging her nose and throat as André had given her all the answer she needed.

Erik was in Paris.

Christine rose to try to regain her composure. "Make haste and bring me home." She followed him silently out of their box praying her shaking wasn't apparent. As soon as the door closed, her trembling worsened. She gripped André for support as the theater police approached.

"Madame la Comtesse, Monsieur le Vicomte. We were sent us to locate you. Monsieur le Comte desires you safely back at *hôtel* Chagny immediately."

A chill ran through her so fast she might as well have been stabbed with an icicle. She nodded. "Immediately then."

Raoul knew something as well. Did she shiver from fear of this impending news, or a misguided shock that Anna Barret had told the truth?

⇢••————•••————••⇠

The carriage that only an hour ago had whisked Christine and André back to *hôtel* Chagny now tripped along the cobblestone streets at a frantic pace, carrying Christine clandestinely away from everything her husband had ordered of her. Stay close to his side? Remain at the townhome? This was not the time for her to curl up like a hedgehog. She recognized Raoul's inherent authority over the situation, but that didn't influence her choice to defy him. The strands of Meyerbeer and her afternoon at the opera seemed like a distant memory as the streets of Paris gave way to the seeder back alleys. The image of Raoul standing behind his desk, wearing his resolve like never before floated ghost-like before her reflection in the carriage window. His resolve was nothing compared to the determination burning Christine's bones.

She swallowed hard when the carriage came to a halt outside a café that looked like its clientele had already been too far down the rabbit hole. She'd heard rumors of Loup frequenting the establishment more than once through the years. Christine prayed he'd be inside, drinking away her husband's stupidity.

Raoul had no idea what he'd done.

As the brougham door opened and the skeptical driver gave her a concerned look, she pressed a small pouch into his hand. "Speak of this to no one."

Leaving the coachman behind to count his coins, Christine moved with purpose toward the café door. As soon as she entered, the sweet aroma of louching absinthe filled her nostrils. It scented the air with excitement; not that drinking was something Christine got excited over. Connoisseurs laughed as they partook in their en vogue rituals making her sigh in relief. The clientele seemed more interested in watching water drip over sugar cubes than in what she was doing there. As she moved among the tables searching the alcohol-enlightened faces around her, her mind spun circles around her dilemma.

She should have smacked sense into Raoul the instant he told her he'd dismissed Loup.

Cutting ties with that hunter wouldn't be that easy.

A sick dread hung overhead as she searched for any sign of Loup. In the café's hearth, flames licked the air mocking her wish that it were the past that could burn away. If only she'd never become subject to Loup's blackmail. Christine boxed away the reminder that any of it was her fault. It was easier to cast blame than take responsibility.

What was she to do? Raoul's fortitude this time around had waved higher than Chagny's standard. Christine never expected that. Loup had all but delivered Erik unto Paris with by his capture of Anna and, now, with André's perplexing sighting at the Garnier; there was no doubt Erik was here. Christine glanced around the café and wandered toward the tables near the hearth. If Raoul were to capture Erik, and she was positive he would, Erik would go to Devil's Island—to his death.

Christine stopped hearthside and touched the mantle. The marble was strikingly cold, but it didn't ease the heat flashing across her neck the more she thought of the idea of Erik hanging by a rope. She couldn't let that happen. She'd sooner die! Faster and faster the years turned in her mind.

By dismissing Loup and cutting him clear of a flow of money from Chagny, Raoul had made it, so nothing would stop the bounty hunter from selling her secrets to the highest paying paper. Did Raoul realize nothing over the years? Money and a reason to hunt were the only things that kept that creature in check. It was why Loup hunted Anna Barret for so many years and took like a dog to the chance for Chagny. Now nothing prevented Loup from ruining Christine's honor and André's future. By cutting Loup off, Raoul had signed their death sentence. There would always be a cloud hovering over Christine's head. The pittance she was already paying Loup to keep silent on her love for Erik wouldn't be nearly enough to satiate his greed now with Changy's money cut off.

"A penny for your thought."

Startled, Christine spun to the table at her right. How had she not seen him there? Loup's beady eyes stared at her over the rim of his glass. He had a glazed look like a man who had just emerged from a long deep sleep.

"I never imagined you crossing into my territory, Comtesse. Dropping your reputation to my level, are you?"

"Keep my reputation out of this." Actually, her reputation had everything to do with this…

"Out of what?" Loup muttered as he slit his eyes and smiled.

"I think you know what." Christine toyed with a ring on her right hand, an elaborate emerald, one of many in her collection, as she swept her gaze around the room.

Loup leaned backward and propped his feet on the table. "You'll need to enlighten me on that. Your husband's stupid decision has me seeing everything through a haze of red and blue." He waved an arm through the air as if swiping away an aura she couldn't see.

Christine's heart barely felt like it had room to beat. She slipped the ring from her finger and slid it across the table. There was more where that came from. Much more. After that, she could promise him the money from what land she could sell.

Loup's jaw cocked as he glanced from the ring to her.

"There is something I need you to do," Christine said.

THIRTEEN

Vahid hated anything higher than an anthill. It took him years to be able to relax on his balcony, let alone a roof.

A mournful wind moaned across the lead of the Opera Garnier's roof while below the lights of Paris gaily twinkled. He must be mad hovering in the doorway like this—let alone doing Erik's bidding all day. Though Vahid wanted to be charmed by those glimmering lights, his legs were shaking with the idea of going any further. Worse, they were dragging him deeper into the clutches of the past. Vahid swore he would someday be free of Erik entirely or able to champion his genius without study or fear. The rooftop door slammed shut behind him, nearly bouncing Vahid off the moon as he stepped fully onto the roof of the Opera Garnier.

It didn't take him long to spot Erik, and Vahid chastised himself for not looking on the rooftop earlier. The monster rose like a massive black bird near the base of Pegasus making Vahid questioned if the Phantom ever really left Paris. Erik moved too calmly. His complete command only meant that his mind rocked with something foreboding. There was no telling if he was studying the city or some manipulative plot in his mind. Panting from his winding climb up ladders and stairs and adrenaline it force-fed him, Vahid's breath shuddered as he surveyed Paris. It remained exquisite except for that blasted new tower.

Genius perhaps, but what a god-awful eyesore.

"Why must you go to extremes, Erik?" His breath coated the air misty white. "If you're not in the bowels of the earth half the time, then you're lurking practically at the sky itself. Which you know I hate. I've been looking everywhere for you."

"Then you have not been looking hard enough, Daroga. I have been sitting like a caged animal around this opera house all day."

Vahid's side cramped. "Forgive me, your highness, for spending the better part of the day wrestling with my conscious over you." It hadn't been an easy battle. It took Vahid hours to decided to deliver that note, knowing what it would set in motion. The only good thing he had done was to leave Erik's boy out of the process.

"I did not ask you to waste time deliberating, Daroga. Did my son deliver my note?"

"*I* delivered your blasted note." If he was able to see Erik's brow, it likely shot up. "I wasn't about to let your son do it."

"Where is he?"

"Safe. I saw Philippe down to your lair hours ago when I returned looking for you. I should have known you'd be up here." Vahid stared off at the Eifel. Looking anyplace else made him certain he'd fall off the roof, no matter how far from the edge he stood. "He was cursing you and your disappearance, by the way. Do you think it was wise to leave them alone down there?"

"The *note*, Daroga."

Erik's tunnel vision was unbelievable. If Vahid had children, they'd be his priority. But then again, Erik never was one to use common sense. Vahid figured most geniuses had that affliction. He studied the way Erik moved. There was something unstable about him. It deepened Vahid's concern. "The comte is ready to gather an army. If you wanted war—you have one. You are about to have all of Paris descend on you, so I suggest you return to your children."

Erik leapt from his spot, his boots clanging loudly on the roof. It sent a charge through Vahid's chest that made him clutch his heart. The way that cloak of his spread around him added to Vahid's illusion of that black bird. Erik's massive form, dark clothing, and mask were countered only by the glow of his eyes. Poe's *Raven* slammed into Vahid's mind. *'Prophet!' said I, 'thing of evil! Prophet still, if bird or devil! Whether tempter sent, or whether tempest tossed thee here ashore…*

"Where is Anna?" Erik demanded. "I will not have the mother of my children kidnapped."

Often, when Erik's voice held that throbbing tone, it was time to fear it. Vahid's lips made a popping sound as he pursed them. "Kidnapped you say? Interesting choice of words. Tell me, Erik, how does that feel?"

"Daroga, you are standing on a rooftop with a man who has a silk rope erotically caressing his right thigh. Do you really want to arouse me right now?"

"You're a fool. Do you have any idea what risk you're putting your children in? Yourself in?"

"I came here to find my Anna. That I have held myself at bay for this long is a miracle. Now, I implore you, before you snap my temper completely in half, where is she?"

Vahid squinted hard as another line from Poe crept into his head. *Desolate yet all undaunted, on this desert land enchanted—on this home by horror haunted—tell me truly, I implore.* "She is at the Chagny townhome." Vahid managed not to flinch as Erik stormed toward him.

"You are blocking my path, Daroga. Be a kind little man and step aside. I came here for Anna, nothing more."

Quoth the raven, 'Nevermore.'

Vahid rubbed at his temple making his scrutiny of the lamplight below waiver. The monster trembled with some unarticulated frustration—Vahid sensed it. It manifested in the slight twitches to Erik's hand. That letter had made matters worse—far worse. He cursed himself for delivering it.

"But you came here with your children!" Vahid's spat made Erik's eyes narrow. Good. It was as much of a punch that Vahid

136

could muster. "You chose to put them first when you took them out of the security of that monastery. You can't run off after Anna half-crazed right now."

Erik touched his temple. He leaned in slightly making Vahid bend backward. "I *am* half-crazed. What would you suggest I do?" With one graceful pounce, he was upon the railing and walking again. Vahid's pulse raced. "My fuse is smoldering and every minute that passes without her is a minute of absolute agony. I am growing angry, Daroga."

"You're not in the position you used to be."

"Daroga—"

"You go running out onto those streets right now after her, and you're as good as dead! You've no idea what will happen to Anna, and if you get yourself killed—" Vahid uneasily eyed Erik's twitching hand. He redirected his approach. "There isn't a shadow in this city that doesn't know the Phantom, regardless of the years that have passed. You've children here to think of, and your state of mind can't handle a thing right now." His eyes shot from Erik's hand to his mask, and back to his hand. Erik balanced precariously on the edge of the rooftop. The wind snapped his cloak sending loops of tension around Vahid's neck. *And the raven, never flitting, still is sitting, still is sitting, On the pallid bust of Pallas just above my chamber door; And his eyes have all the seeming of a demon's that is dreaming.* Vahid clenched his jaw and shoved his thoughts aside. He didn't believe he was about to say what was on his mind and entrench himself in Erik's business even more, but it was better than unleashing him on Paris. "You stay here. I'll return to the comte and attempt to leave with Anna." Erik's eyes shifted abruptly, moved, and glowed at him from an even higher spot. Vahid spun searching high and low for his evaporating specter. "You can't have the control when you're the one in danger of losing it. Don't do anything stupid. Do you hear me, Erik? Stay burrowed like the mole you are until I come to you to let you know all is clear. You have children to consider, you colossal fool!"

A disembodied voice surged like a rising tide and floated menacingly around him.

"Get off my roof, Daroga."

Those words died on the wind and the slam of the rooftop door. Erik stared at the back of Vahid's head until he had disappeared resigned to stay 'burrowed' for only so long. By the time he made it from the rooftop back to his labyrinth, he had replayed the daroga's criticism a thousand times in his head. His words only raised his impatience a notch higher and made the time that had past since he arrived yesterday more abrasive for Erik. The comte had best obey his note and show himself. Erik had waited long enough already. He was trying to best to hold his temper without shedding blood. It was for the sake of his children that he didn't charge Raoul down the instant he arrived in Paris. The thought of the daroga taking charge of a situation that Erik should command was a bitter pill to swallow. However, the daroga had a point. Erik couldn't let his children suffer the consequences of his wrath.

Nor could he ignore the ear-numbing silence in his labyrinth once he made it back down there. Gone was the constant music of Simone's violin, and Philippe was nowhere to be found. Their names died as echoes for the third time. Erik left them only so long as to collect his thoughts on the roof, yet time wasn't exactly something of which he was cognizant.

"Philippe? Simone!"

Realizing they were gone, Erik's face heated; the backs of his hands tightened, and his stomach clenched. Gone, like Anna. His ineptitude in all this had reached his children. The Dargoa was right. Kicking out his rage, Erik sent the organ bench sliding into the far wall. He turned away from the destroyed seat and leaned hard on the organ cabinet, fighting the urge to rip each stop out as if they were thorns embedded in his side. The world above moved at its precious pace while he remained far below ground. He'd rendered himself powerless when he should take over and let himself loose on the world.

Erik squeezed his eyes trying to deaden the noisc in his mind. First, he failed Anna, and now his children. He couldn't afford to have his mind fail him now too. That seemed impossible when sounds and thoughts kept creeping in on him, stealing any chance he had to breathe without being aware that something sinister gnawed on this mind. To his side, an ancient clock sat like a neglected, wicked, time thief. Hating the thought of the seconds that laughed at him as they ticked by, he picked up a brass paperweight and launched it at the clock's face. It shattered, but his tension didn't.

Erik stared into his weak reflection in the fractured glass around his feet. A confounded manhunt and an inescapable past had dominion over him right now. Somewhere several stories above, likely on the street alone and disoriented, were his children, while Chagny held Anna against her will.

His black-mask reflected a gloomy gray at him. Erik curled his fingers to his mask until the edges bit mercilessly against his cheeks.

He should remain buried as the daroga said, in case the children return. He should stay below ground and keep them safe. The best thing to do was to allow people to help him. He should allow the daroga time. But then again, he should pick up a shard of glass and try to cut apart every person that stood in his way. While he was at it, he should cut out every aspect of his life that went wrong.

Yes, Erik should stay buried. Erik should have stayed buried from the very start!

Erik grabbed his head. Damn Philippe de Chagny and his meddling! If not for him Erik would not have his children or Anna. He wouldn't need them. He wouldn't feel this agitating guilt for failing them. Erik's body curled forward as if being burned alive. The noise in his head was all could hear.

His life had come full circle. He sat in solitude below an opera house planning his next move against Raoul de Chagny, while the world above him was oblivious. From one extreme to the next, Erik rocked with thoughts he could understand and thoughts he couldn't understand. When the image of his peaceful life in Germany tore Erik's memories at the seams, he jerked his fingers off his mask. His cold fingertips grew oddly warm with newly moving blood. He flexed his hands then clenched them again, the motion helping to pump more force behind his scream.

"Anna!"

Madness surged. It spread like cancer. He was going insane without her and being back in the opera house, so close to where his nightmares began, was triggering reactions and memories he couldn't suppress. Erik was slipping into persona's he didn't want to revisit. His eyes rolled back freeing himself from his reflection in the shattered glass, and allowing him to give in to the noise in his mind. Air heaved in and out of his vacant nose. Sweat trickled down his neck and dampened the collar of his shirt. He had to end this ridiculous farce.

"By any means necessary."

His rage sent the already shattered clock careening down his drawing room stairs. He would end it if it killed him. End it for the sake of his son's gifts and Simone's precious outlook on the world. His children were now gone, and his last scrap of sanity was holding on by a steadily fraying strand.

"By any and all means!"

An intense calm washed over him with each heaving breath that filled his lungs. Looking around his underground lair, Erik knew without a doubt that he no longer belonged in this realm. He was master of another life and wouldn't remain buried like the dead. Not when he lived and could end this manhunt in the way he knew how. He couldn't protect his children without them, and he was nothing to them without their mother.

The daroga would not return to *hôtel* de Chagny and leave with Anna.

He would.

The time had come. As a Phantom or man, the time had come.

The Persian had been wrong about one thing. Erik was not as good as dead if he ventured out. The streets of Paris had been oblivious to him. Though the citizens of Paris may have been ignorant of Erik, every street and building that he had past rammed some sound or echo into his mind. It was just as years past when a Phantom had completely taken over his life and Erik didn't know where he ended, and his darker side began. He did his best to stay focused on the task at hand and label the noise in his mind for what it was. Erik had prowled the streets as if he owned them, keeping to alleys and shadows until he was ensconced in the Chagny townhome. He'd known for decades prior where it stood, and he regretted not charging down the doors the instant he arrived in Paris. The Chagny townhome stood as ignorant to him being near as the Garnier had years ago.

Slipping inside through the hustle of the busy servant's entrance had been child's play. Rounding himself through corridors and rooms unseen came naturally to him. So much so, Erik thought perhaps he should have seeped into the hallowed halls of Chagny itself years ago and ended all this then. Better yet, he should have delivered his note himself and ripped the house down brick by brick until Chagny's presence in his life was nothing more than rubble and dust.

Erik paused and centered his breathing thinking perhaps it would help focus him. Far from it. Fresh floor polish and scent of the hallway bouquets only made it more evident that this manhunt had robbed his family of the comfort they deserved. Erik stood behind a marble column and scanned the main hall. Anna had to be somewhere in the main house. She wasn't below stairs where anyone like her ought to be. He found that strange. What game was Chagny playing?

Erik studied an ornate door at the far end of a hall then glanced to the two footmen stationed conspicuously outside a salon on the opposite end. Why would footmen need to be flanking a closed door? Erik felt his blood quicken. Anna had to be there. Moving from column to column, he pressed himself flat behind the one closest to the salon. The manipulation of his ventriloquism was all it took to make the footmen turn toward the "distraught" voice coming from behind the door. When they moved to investigate, Erik stealthily followed. He pirouetted into the room and behind the open doors out of sight before ever seeing if Anna was there.

"What is it you need? You called out," a footman barked.

Erik nodded and held his breath. So someone *was* in there.

"No, I didn't," came the reply. "But since you asked, how long does the comte plans on keeping me here?"

Erik knew the annoyed clip to that voice. He closed his eyes and forced himself to remain calm, though every muscle wanted to leap toward Anna. A distant servants bell rang making him jump. Erik froze as he heard footsteps approach the door he hid behind.

"Don't call out again." The second footman snapped as he and the other moved out the door and toward the sound of the jangling bell.

"Even if I did the first time, I'd do it again if I pleased," Anna shouted as they passed through the doors. "Idiots."

Anna's blunt reply coursed blood through Erik's veins, and if he were a believing man, he'd thank that God of hers that she still had spirit in her. He waited until the footmen slammed the door shut to round out from behind it. Looking at her as she stood there, back to him and head bowed, he felt the veil between sanity and madness start to divide. Anna had that power over him. She was the antidote to the racket in his mind that, if left unchecked, always threatened to overpower him.

"If I am dreaming," he whispered hoarsely, "then do not wake me and if you are a ghost then let me die right now."

Anna's head yanked up. She spun around. "Erik?"

Catching her small frame mid-leap as she charged forward and launched herself at him, Erik crushed her to his chest. He held her tightly, trying to force her very essence into his heart. Lowering her back to the ground only caused that veil to ripple, and not wanting to hear the noise in his mind again, he pulled her back. From arm's length to his chest again, he battled with holding on and letting go to do what he knew he must. Sane or mad, he needed her, and this farce had to end. How could he have allowed them to steal her? When he finally released her, his despair turned to anger.

Her face. "Who touched you?" Erik growled.

Anna glanced frantically to the door and shushed him silent. "Hush! Loup. The comte dismissed him. There's no telling where he is. There won't be much time before he turns on

Chagny. We must get out of here. But those footmen..."

Erik's stare had clamped on the colors on her cheek. His hands shot forward. They roamed up and down her naked neck and raked through her short locks. If he tried to twist her braid around his wrist, he would have been weaving air.

He pawed at her shoulders, her waist, and up again searching for any sign of harm. "What else? What else did he do to you? This is all by Loup? *Loup*?" Her meek nod and fresh tears spoke volumes.

Panicked, Anna pressed a hand to his mouth. "Erik, slow down. We'll leave. Gather the children and flee. The Persian was here this morning. He said he'd tell you and the children where I was. Where are they? Are they alright?"

The children? It was for the children Erik was going to channel all he felt over this manhunt once and for all. His face contorted as if his thoughts were a weapon. All emotion and regret left his voice. "Anna, do you still love me?"

"There was never a moment I didn't." She snatched his hands. "Come. Get us out of here. Let's go to the children and leave."

Erik didn't budge. He gently pressed his finger to her lips. He stroked them as if caressing the delicate wings of a butterfly. "It is too late to leave.

"Please, Erik, we must." She tugged his sleeve to try to get him to move.

"No, Anna. The noise will not go away."

Anna stopped tugging. She knew the implication. "Noise."

Though she said the word as fact and not a question, Erik nodded in confirmation. His breath hitched as she laid a hand on his mask. The heat of her hand seeped through the thin leather, and although the tumult of every emotion already flushed him, her warmth was calming.

"All will be well, Erik. You *can* slow down."

Erik lifted his hand and laid it against hers. She'd been telling him such for years now. He was lured back to the first time she had shouted that to him in the cellars of the opera house. The words had a way of shocking him into reorganizing his thoughts.

But this time they only calmed him so much.

"No. Slowing down will not help anymore. My fate, it is as if it is lurking, re-awakening and—" He looked to the window where beyond lay the dome of the Opera Garnier. "—being played upon Apollo's Lyre."

Erik moved his hand off of hers and proceeded to stroke her cheek. He attempted to brush the concern and confusion away from her. Erik kept his caress as light as he could so as not to hurt her further.

"I am so very, very angry, Anna. I am the Phantom. It is all I ever was." He stared into the emotion swimming in her eyes and felt his throat constrict.

Anna tried to silence him by pressing her tear-coated kiss to his, but Erik wouldn't have it. Shaking her off was fruitless though. Her kiss sucked him out of the murk in his mind. He let her take over control of the moment since he knew soon she would have none. Anna's soft lips drugged him, and for the brief moment she kissed him, he gave in to the high. He curled her deeper into the crook of his arm seeking shelter in her understanding and retreat in the powerful responses her body awakened in him.

Though he held her, it was Erik who clung hard to keep from falling.

Breaking their kiss, they listened to the silence that deadened the room.

"Where are our children, Erik?" Anna whispered. "Phantom or not, I want to take you home."

The sound of her voice should have continued as the drug that soothed his rotting mind, but instead, in breaking the kiss, he had said his good-bye.

"We are not going home. I can no longer allow my past to be an outworn history in our lives. It is a wound that continues to bleed. Anna, I love you more than music itself. There is no melody to match the beauty you have brought me, but I end this now. My way."

"Where… where are they? Please? Erik?"

Her voice shook. His heart trembled more.

"I don't know, but I will find them, and this will end."

Erik knew he'd confused her with those words, but he had no time to address them. As silence increased, the concern behind her eyes intensified. Erik was sitting on the edge of so many things, the edge of fury, desire, ecstasy, and danger. He closed his eyes and allowed himself to give into the noise, releasing himself to fall over the edge of all of them.

FOURTEEN

The muscles of his cheek jumped the tighter Philippe clenched his jaw.

He was not a lying beggared, and the servant accusing him of such was in danger of having his teeth knocked out if he didn't permit them at least through the threshold. Simone shivered against his leg as chilly blasts of air knifed them in the back. He was thankful he had the presence of mind to keep his sister's hood up, and her face tipped to the floor, thus sparing the Chagny townhome a horrific awakening, but he was thinking better of it now. Perhaps scaring the daylights out of the insufferable footman would get him to move faster.

Philippe shoved the vicomte's card hard against the man's chest. He was about to yank down the bell he rang and smash him over the head with it.

"Did you not hear me correctly the first two times? My name is Philippe Georges Marie."

Philippe's eyes bored blood draining holes into the servant's back when he finally left, card in gloved hand. Though he was left waiting only a few minutes, it seemed like hours before the man returned and escorted them to the drawing room with word that the comtesse and vicomte would attend them soon.

That tension in his jaw threatened to overtake his entire body. Massaging his eyes until he saw stars, Philippe paced the richly appointed room trying hard not to study the ornate trimmings he saw through the tiny pinpricks of light now dancing in his vision. Red and blue hues stirred to life giving the room an inviting air. *Nothing of this is inviting. Nothing, nothing, nothing. Mein Gott, Simone.*

A huff of annoyance popped out his mouth. Stilling Simone's arm for a fourth time as he passed her, he forced her to lower the instrument from her chin.

"Whatever you want to say right now it can wait. I don't want to hear it," he grumbled.

Simone drew the bow across the strings and made the violin shriek loudly. Philippe flinched. He took it to mean she was less than pleased with him at the moment. That's all he needed right now.

"Simone. If you have something to say to me, use words."

The rings he saw below her eyes as she glared at him in reply nearly forced his fist through the closest wall more than once. Instead, his pressed his palms against a waist-high table and breathed deeply. The aroma of roses filled his nose but didn't calm him. How could they when Simone was inching her violin under her chin again.

"Simone, I want out of this just as much as you do. I want our mother and father back and everything to be normal again. I know you don't understand, but just, please… stop."

His chin sagged to his chest. She was softly tapping the bow to the strings like a child dancing with a need to relieve herself. He rolled his head toward her and gave up. Who was he to stop her?

"Fine. Play. Rattle bones for all I care. This entire situation is such a mess it might as well be set to music."

"You test me in extraordinary means, Daroga."

The tip of his walking stick clicked off his impatience as

Raoul attempted to finish a mind-clearing walk. The instant he'd run into the Persian making his way toward the Chagny townhome as well thwarted that attempt. There was a chill to the evening air, and it made Raoul pick up his pace the closer he got. The Persian, spry for his old age, had kept up no matter how much Raoul had zigzagged and delayed his route home to avoid him. Erik's note, damp from the mist, crumbled as Raoul rammed it back into his waistcoat pocket.

"Rightful you should shove that away finally," the Persian said. "What were you doing? Walking around just staring at it? That will do nothing to change the fact that history is repeating."

"Did you return here merely to state the obvious, Daroga? I should have you arrested for stalking."

"I returned to knock sense into you. The only rational thing you've done is dismiss that lack-whit bounty hunter. You speak now of running off to the Opera Garnier in search of Erik?"

Raoul stopped. "You read that note. Erik wants an audience with me. He'll get one at the Garnier. I fail to believe he isn't here."

"You're a gentleman, not an investigator! I've sent you to opera houses across the world for legitimate reasons, but think of it. A criminal never returns to the scene of his crimes. It's madness. I already searched the Opera house. I told you. It remains as it was."

Raoul tossed his head back and laughed before he resumed walking. "As if I believe any of that."

"To go there now is wasted time. Prudence is the way, Monsieur. Let professionals deal with tracking Erik and release Mademoiselle Barret to me. Let me get the answers out of her that you need."

Raoul stopped mid-jog up the broad steps of his residence. Professionals hadn't helped him get to the end of this manhunt in years. "You don't understand that I don't trust you do you, Daroga? I don't trust anyone any longer." He tapped him dead center of his chest with the tip of his stick preventing him from following up the stairs. "For years you sat on the outskirts of everything and now you're more than willing to offer advice and assistance? I don't trust anyone to take care of anything relating to the Phantom but me." The door opened as if on cue. Raoul marched inside, speaking to the daroga who breezed in behind him, as his staff relieved him of his coat and hat. "Your constant badgering to release the girl to your custody only raises my suspicions over your involvement."

His tension wound higher when he spied Christine and André at the far end of the hall moving as if part of a funeral march. Legard hastened his way forward ahead of them.

Raoul slid his waistcoat aside and put a hand on his hip. He flicked the footman away. "What is it, Legard? Everyone looks like they are under a blasted dark cloud and I don't mean the one that has been following me." He jerked a thumb toward the Persian. His wife and son paused outside the distant doors to the drawing room. André had slid a hand to her shoulder. "Is it Christine?" Raoul lowered his voice. "André?"

"Quite the opposite," Legard replied. "While you were gone an unprecedented guest arrived to call on Chagny. The staff alerted me immediately. We were about to visit the drawing room."

Something was off. He knew Legard. The man was as straightforward as an arrow. "All of you? So I assume it isn't the Phantom." Christine appeared paler the closer Raoul got.

"No. It's Philippe Georges Marie."

Raoul stopped short making the Persian nearly slammed into his back. For a second Raoul's heart inverted as the image of his brother's flag-draped coffin came to mind. In another second he felt it skip a beat in a fantasy that his brother was alive.

"I find no humor in that, Legard," he said, voice as serious as he could make it, once he'd gathered his thoughts back into line.

"Neither do I," the daroga echoed cautiously.

Raoul schooled his features and addressed Christine and his son. "Whatever the meaning of this is, I want both of you to disregard it. I'll not have one thing upsetting either of you. André?"

His son had a strange expression; like that of a child expecting the worst punishment.

Raoul's hand stopped on the drawing room doorknob before he could address his son's look further. The air around them hummed with sweet but strangely unnerving music. Raoul warned everyone to mind their place with one glance before he shoved open the door.

What in all of Heaven...

A gasp leapt from Christine's mouth. Raoul pulled her protectively aside.

A small child, back to them, stood on his ottoman in the center of the room. The youth to her side pushed off the side table and snapped to attention. He bowed respectfully. Lifting his hand in an elegant move that could have come from the most accomplished maestro, he bade the girl be silent. The child didn't turn around. She merely lowered her violin and stared out the window.

"What is the meaning of this," Raoul insisted as Legard and the Persian pushed forward behind him. He released Christine to Legard. "You've some nerve to enter this home young man and disrespect the name of a very powerful comte. Whoever you are I suggest you start telling the truth for I will not have Chagny treated in such an egregious manner."

"What disrespect, Monsieur? I enter this home by invitation of your vicomte."

"My vicomte?" Raoul shot a look at André whose face had gone tight. Raoul noted the turmoil behind his eyes.

"I am Philippe Georges Marie, and lies are pointless. They only breed scandal, and I tend to dislike scandal."

That phrased cut across the air like a challenger's glove. The boy sounded precisely like the note's author. It raised his suspicion.

"I won't be played with," Raoul warned. "Give me your entire name before I have you arrested and escorted out of here."

"I lack a surname, and we're not going anywhere until you answer our questions about our mother's whereabouts."

The little girl hopped off the ottoman and turned.

Nothing prepared Raoul for what he saw. Nothing.

His heart raced as if he ran for miles. Shock billowed around Christine as her dainty hands trembled like a fallen leaf in front of her lips. Legard had slammed his eyes shut and turned away, his thumb and forefinger pinching the bridge of his nose. André averted his eyes as well, gripping his mother's arm and staring at the floor. An icy chill flashed across Raoul's body. There was no looking away from the abomination before him. The little girl stared up at him, her bizarre eyes studying him as openly as he did her.

"*Guten Tag,*" she chirped.

She cocked her head curiously and clutched the violin to her chest as Raoul backed away. The innocent expression skewed her face into a macabre oxymoron. Instinctually, Raoul positioned himself between his wife and son. The Persian didn't flinch.

"You move as though we're a threat, Monsieur le Comte." Philippe draped his hand across the girl's shoulders. "Simone is merely a child, and I would thank you not to look on her as if she were a monster."

Raoul filled his burning lungs and let the air seep out tightly clenched teeth. He never dreamed he would grind out his next words. "Where is your father?"

"Where my father is, isn't the question. The question is regarding our mother. Did you take her? Because you shouldn't have, she is innocent. Isn't that right, Comtesse?"

Like a match to a powder keg chain reactions exploded around the room. Christine's stammers bounced down Raoul's spine while André's fervor that his mother be respected resulted in Raoul holding him back with a quick block of his arm.

"Enough!" Raoul commanded. "Your father is solely responsible for everything, and I'll have you confirm for me *right now*, his whereabouts. I assure you no harm or blame will come to you or that girl."

"*That* girl? Her name is Simone. You dare blame my family for this ridiculous manhunt when the entire thing could end with one confession from your wife?"

Raoul forced his hand harder against the thoroughbred that had replaced his son.

"You will treat the Comtesse de Chagny with respect she is due young man," Legard interjected.

"A liar begets no respect, Monsieur le Comte," Philippe spat. "My parents saved her life. She's well aware. Inquire such of the daroga." The boy pointed toward the Persian. "He told me everything."

Raoul's nostrils flared. He took two strides toward Philippe. "You will leave the Comtesse de Chagny out of this and tell me his whereabouts immediately. Chagny will not be threatened by him or disrespected by you."

"My father isn't a threat to anyone. He is—"

"A murderer and a manipulative madman!"

The air erupted with intense music. It cut down Raoul's words as if they were a saber through butter. An agonizing tune arched wildly out Simone's violin filling the room as if a thousand voices screamed in unison. Crazy-eyed, she leaning against her strings, her fingers flying faster with each passing second.

"Simone," Philippe cried, but she didn't respond. "Simone!"

She backed herself farther toward a corner making the violin shriek with pitches so fast and so varied it was difficult to concentrate.

"For the love of God, make her stop!" Raoul shouted, his ears ringing painfully.

Christine clutched her temples. "What possesses her? Raoul! Legard! Daroga!"

"Dear Lord, is she mad?" Legard exclaimed, rubbing viciously at his earlobe.

"She isn't mad!" Philippe yelled over the din. "You've upset her. You did this to her! *You've hurt my sister!*" Swinging his back to them, he knelt before Simone, ducking her bow arm several times before he managed to seize it and bring the music to a screeching halt. "It's alright," he cooed. "Calm down; I'm here. They won't hurt you."

Raoul jerked his fingers off his ears. The note in his pocket practically burned a hole into his chest. "If Erik is anywhere," he replied sharply, "he's at that opera house." Raoul marched toward the boy and shoved the note into Philippe's hands. A powerful current coursed between them. "I should have acted on my instinct far sooner and ignored the suggestions of the Persian. Your father is what I say. And we end this now. Angels of Music do not exist, madmen do."

FIFTEEN

"Are you so certain of that, Monsieur?"

The words leveled the room like a bolt of lightning shocking everyone in their place. Erik whispered for Anna to stay in the doorway even though it pained him to see her agony as soon as she laid eyes on her children. He crossed the room, circling where Raoul stood and called to his son.

"Philippe."

Knowing that tone and command by heart, the boy curled a protective arm around his sister, who still shook, dazed and confused over what she had just played. Only Christine's voice lifted the lid of the coffin-like stillness.

"My God. Erik."

He had tried not to look at her, more concerned by the painful strains of Simone's music that had led him from the salon to her side, but now he had no choice. He forced himself to look directly at her. Seeing Christine and hearing her voice—his sweet drug of years past—drained the air from his lungs. He closed his eyes for a second and studied the afterglow of her image in the darkness. The moment was fleeting though. Erik wouldn't give in to that drug any longer. He came here to do one thing, and he would see it through to completion.

Erik opened his eyes and with a determined stare looked at Legard, the Persian, and an extraordinary youth to Christine's side. "Monsieur le Vicomte, I presume?"

The boy didn't have to reply. The way he stood, the attitude he projected, and even the facial ticks he had as he tried to compose himself made him look strikingly like his father. The vicomte reached for his mother in the same way Raoul did as Christine inched closer to them.

"Still inwardly uncertain of the Angel of Music after all these years, Christine, or are you seeking comfort some other reason?" Erik didn't wait to read her for a response. "It matters if not. The past will soon be over."

Erik turned his attention to his children as he paced the center of the wide circle the gathered crowd had created. He watched every one of them with each rotation knowing that circling wouldn't settle his thoughts—acting on them would. Erik paused in front of Raoul. "It has been a while, Monsieur le Comte, have you nothing to say?"

"I'll say everything I need when they cast your sentence."

"Impressive. You have found a backbone after all these years."

"Have your say before I have you arrested."

Erik chuckled at the threat and acted as if he was going to begin circling again. "My sentence you say?" He took one step away from Raoul before whirling around. He hooked Raoul's neck with one arm, swinging him away from Christine and cutting off Raoul's command for Legard to stand by her.

"Stand down, Monsieur Legard, and reach for that pistol not an inch more! I will have my say, or I will end this in a manner I wish *not!*" Legard spread his arms and nodded. The Persian had the presence of mind move closer to Philippe and Simone while Anna remained frozen in the doorway. Erik turned his attention back to the man bucking in his arms.

"My sentence," he hissed into Raoul's ear, "has already been cast." Erik tore off his mask and shoved it hard against Raoul's face, satisfied with how it made him writhe. "Look through it, damn you! Is it tight? Hot? Do you feel that biting along its edge?

That outline around the eyes?" Erik pressed it harder every time Raoul tried to fling it off. "It is always there; it never goes away." Erik wrenched Raoul higher forcing him to the tips of his toes making the comte grunt. "However, when I take this mask off, you have instant freedom."

Springing his hand open, Erik tore the mask away and shoved Raoul aside, freeing him from his arms and the black-masked prison. The comte staggered before looking up at Erik, then away.

"See what I mean?" Erik snarled. "All these years later and you still cannot look at me. I can remove the mask but the face is still there, and you have made it so no matter where I go the two cannot be separate. Because of you no matter where *we* went, the past was there to greet us."

"Are you trying to play the victim, Erik?" Raoul had pulled himself up straight and lifted his chin like a battle-ready rebel. It disgusted Erik that he made any attempt to look formidable.

"The victims are my children."

"What?" Raoul had that indignant air about him. Erik nodded. That was more the Raoul he knew.

"My son, Philippe Georges Marie," Erik explained, walking the circle and stopping in front of the boy, "was born in an abandoned barn somewhere between here and Germany." For a moment he let his voice grow as distant as the memory as he held his son's gaze. There was confusion behind Philippe's crystal blue eyes, a confusion Erik would not soon forget. He broke the stare and glared at Raoul. "I laid Anna down on a filthy horse blanket out of the way of the leaking roof, and vermin, and delivered him myself because there was no midwife around who did not know my face."

"What does that have to do with the life of a liar and murder?" Raoul clipped. "You orchestrated your despicable destiny, not I."

"My daughter," Erik continued loudly to prove he was not to be interrupted, "was born in a small village that she dearly misses." If Philippe's confused look cut Erik that sharply, then Simone's was about to divide him in two. Erik reached out and stroked her hair mouthing that he loved her in German so that she'd have something of a comfort to cling to. He tried not to feel his guilt when he continued in French. "She feels safe there, but because of how this manhunt has made the world fear this," turning back to Raoul he pointed at his face, "and how you have made certain that *my* past is attached to it, my little girl lives in fear of the day she will receive her mask." There could be no heavier words to say when speaking of Simone. Erik somberly returned the mask to his face. "I can see it in her eyes. She has been condemned enough. I will not have children a part of this any longer. They are too young to spend their lives looking over their shoulders because of a past they did not create. I cannot give Christine what she needs to end this insanity, but I can give you what you want."

"What is it Christine wants?" Raoul gave her a fleeting glance before returning his scrutiny to Erik.

Incredulous, Erik walked the circle back to Raoul. "Could you be married to her all these years and not know?"

"I'm fully aware of the command you still have over her."

"My power over her was severed years ago. It is the command she has over you that you refuse to see; my question is, what is this doing to your son? If she cannot completely love you does she completely love him?"

"You bastard!"

Raoul's left hook shot out as a sideways blur as his fist cracked across Erik's jaw. Erik jerked to the side as he took that punch and suppressed every fiber that screamed at him to react.

"What is it you're doing, Erik?" Raoul demanded.

Erik rubbed his jaw, as he tasted blood. He ignored the pain but couldn't ignore the noise ringing perversely in his ears. "Ending this. I am through with giving in to a madman. I lived in solitude thinking this was behind us and I had finally been rewarded with some small scrap of normalcy. However, so long as the past is perpetuated my family will never be free. Ending it cannot come on your end, because if it could, this would have been over years ago. So I end this manhunt now. Do what you want with me; just leave my family in peace."

Raoul almost laughed. "Peace? The Phantom speaks of

peace? How do I know those are not words you are throwing me before you strike me down right here?"

Face-to-face with his nemesis, Erik slowly shook his head knowing he could take a strand of silk rope out of his pocket and kill Raoul before anyone's next blink. "If I wanted to kill you, I would have done it a thousand times over already, but I promised your brother I would not."

Raoul flinched.

"You will never live up to the man he was, so cringe when I mention him all you want," Erik spat. "Make your choice. Either you trust the years where you *never* saw me, or you do not, and you cut me down. Let me rot in prison for all it will spare my family. However, I suggest you act now. You are trying my patience, and I am losing my will for control."

"He tries *your* patience? How bloody quaint."

Anna's shriek stopped them in their tracks as Loup's words faded into his deranged laughter. All eyes shot to the door and the pistol he had pressed tightly to Anna's forehead. Erik's heart lodged in his throat.

"What did you expect? That some damn nobleman would tell me what I can and cannot do? That I would slink away without taking her?" Loup moved into the room forcing Anna to move with him. Her feet shuffled along the floor in front of him; her hands clung tightly to the arm Loup had clamped around her neck. As he laughed and that pistol ground against her temple, her eyes filled with a soul-diminishing fear. From where he stood, Erik could hear Anna's breath shaking out of her mouth, sounding like dry bones tumbling from a sack to the marble floor. Bouncing just on top of the sound of her fear was Philippe's whisper for his mother, so chilling that it could have frozen the air.

Blind and malevolent hatred flared within Erik. As soon as he lunged forward, the pistol twisted, and Anna's cry rang perversely in his ears. Erik stopped short, his heart pounding out the size of Anna's fear.

"One move!" Loup shouted. "Make one more move, and I swear I will level your pretty little Anna before your eyes. A bullet can be triggered faster than a Phantom, you idiot. Don't tempt me." Loup spun he and Anna toward Legard whose hand had stopped as it hovered over the pistol at his hip. "Any of you." As Legard held his hands away from his sides and backed off, Loup sucked Anna's earlobe into his mouth. It made a popping sound when he released it.

Erik's fury billowed.

"Forgive me for interrupting your conversation," Loup said. "Now with all of you under my gun, I've all I need to control this charade. While it's been fun playing games with Chagny over who would pay me more for the Phantom—the comte or comtesse—oh please, now is not the time to look so baffled, Monsieur le Comte. She came running to find me the instant you dismissed me. Promised me double what you paid to keep Erik *out* your reach this time around! In addition to the money she's been paying me to keep her love for him a secret from you, how could I refuse?"

Erik slid his eyes off of Anna only long enough to watch Christine invent a new shade of white. As Christine's breath hitched and she looked to Raoul, Erik noted his lips disappear to a tight line beneath his mustache.

"You lying manipulative bastard." Raoul's voice was as deadly as Erik felt.

Loup shrugged as if Raoul's tone was a bothersome flea. "However having the Phantom show up *here* takes all the fun out of that cat and mouse game for me and we can't have that now, can we? I only returned to collect what is mine," Loup tapped Anna's temple with the pistol, "and it seems we now have a problem."

Keeping Anna's head locked in the jaws of his arm, Loup swung the pistol directly at Raoul. Christine screamed, flinging herself into her husband's arms seconds before her knees gave out beneath her. Raoul shielded her with his body as his they twisted to the floor.

"You insane dog!" Raoul shouted his body hunched protectively over Christine.

Loup aimed low. "If she was thinking to shield you, then she's stupid. A bullet can pass through two people. Now, pay me what you owe me. It seems you dismissed me without doing that. Remember a bullet flies fast and straight, and only I know the target. Either I get my money, or someone will die." Loup moved the pistol from Raoul, back to Anna's temple, and then back to Raoul. "No reply? Suit yourself."

The pistol trigger cocked igniting enough murder in Erik for a legion of men. Chaos flooded the room as Erik's rage rang loud. Just over his roar were the fearful screams of his children as widespread panic whipped around the room in the time it took that pistol to cock. Christine's scream rent the air as Raoul shielded her from the inevitable. While Erik sprung toward Loup, he barely heard Raoul's command for Legard to shoot or the Persian's scream of 'no!'

Two shots crossed in the air.

And the world stopped spinning.

SIXTEEN

The metallic scent of blood replaced the sharp, sweet smell of cordite in the air.

With the boom of the gunshots still ringing in his ears, a superhuman cry of rage clawed its way out of Erik. He launched himself past Legard and his pistol toward Loup and his. The hunter turned the weapon toward Erik's oncoming blur, flinging Anna aside in the process, but Erik saw nothing other than red.

In seconds, a blood-stopping crunch crackled around them as Erik's grief wrenched the bones apart in Loup's neck. Erik's hands sprung open, and the bounty hunter dropped to the floor with a lifeless thud at his feet. The silence that followed stood so thick even the human heart questioned its right to beat.

Anna backed off, swimming with her arms and legs away from where she was thrown and the grotesque expression and lifeless eyes of Loup. She rolled over and crawled hand-over-hand toward the other body on the floor. Erik staggered as well to the motionless bundle that lay silently between him, Anna, Raoul, and Christine.

"Simone? Si—Simone?" First one knee then the next hit the floor as the full weight of the moment hit Erik in the chest. "Simone?"

Tiny ringlets fanned across her temples. Beside her feet, her beloved violin and bow lay silent. Her eyes were closed, her breathing barely there. He stroked the hair from her face, terrified at the crimson spreading across her dress and pooling on the floor. He rocked, back and forth over her not knowing what to touch or where to go. Dazed, he pressed his palm against the blood on her chest, not entirely sure what he was seeing.

When he screamed, Paris recoiled.

Erik staggered to his feet and stumbled drunkenly toward Raoul, who hovered stock-still over Christine. "My little girl! My little girl!" Erik swayed like a drunkard as he stared at his red-coated hand. "Who... who shot... who shot...?"

Christine gripped Raoul until she was white knuckled. Anna's whimpers jerked Erik's head toward her. She clung glassy-eyed and open-mouthed, one arm around Philippe's leg the other around the Persian's. She looked ash-gray. Erik staggered back to where he had been and dropped to the floor again. He struggled to lift Simone into his arms. A child that was once so light suddenly felt immeasurably heavy. He shook so violently he could barely get a grip on her.

Winded, Legard pushed his way through him. Erik stared up at him, his eyes locking on his now holstered gun. "Give her to me," Legard insisted as Erik's eyes carved a path up Legard's legs.

"Who shot... who shot...?"

"Let me have her," Legard demanded. "Erik, please!"

Erik shook his head in a confused daze, desperately clinging to Simone's body as Legard dropped to one knee to pry her of his grip. An incomprehensible sound ground out of Erik's throat as he used his grief and shock to ram Legard aside with his shoulder. Erik clung tighter to Simon's motionless body as Legard refused to stand-down.

"You must release her to me!" Legard ordered, breaking Erik's white-knuckled grip finger-by-finger until his hands slipped off Simone's body and hung useless at his sides. Erik watched Simone's head fall lax against Legard's shoulder as he gathered the child into his arms. Rising, Legard rushed toward the door only stopping when Raoul's hand shot up and grabbed the hem of his waistcoat.

"Whatever it takes, Jules. You use whatever I have. You drain my accounts; you sell Chagny, you sell my soul! Whatever it takes, do not return and tell me that little girl has died."

It is to the credit of human nature, that, except where its selfishness is brought into play, it loves more readily than it hates. Hatred, by a gradual and quiet process, will even be transformed to love, unless the change be impeded by a continually new irritation of the original feeling of hostility.

~Nathaniel Hawthorne, The Scarlet Letter

SEVENTEEN

Nothing was deeper or darker than the grief found in questioning the outcome of the unknown. Try as one may to control the unpredictable, the only partner to grief was time. Sometimes it healed. At other times, like now, time stood as a faceless, nameless presence that couldn't be turned back. Like a curious pilgrim, perpetual queries wandered in Raoul's mind for answers he didn't possess until his thoughts had him twisted around so well he hardly recognized himself.

"He was turning himself over to me, Christine," Raoul muttered. She stood at his side, but he kept his forearms on his thighs and his eyes on his boots. "And a child pays the price."

Christine didn't reply. Part of him didn't want her to. Not with the questions dragging across his mind. The door at the far end of the hall opened. Collectively the group gathered in the small waiting area of a Paris hospital sucked in a breath—but Raoul released his in a slow, steady stream. He tapped his son's thigh and stood. André sat stoically next to him; his head hung low between his arms. Erik stood at the far window, back to them all,

Legard and his Inspectors cautiously close behind. Anna was curled in a chair, near catatonic in her stares as her son and the Persian stood vigil over her.

It was Raoul's manhunt that brought them here, and he felt the weight of that burn behind his eyes.

"It's difficult," the doctor explained. "She hasn't regained consciousness yet from the surgery. I would be lying if I didn't mention the possibility that she never will, not a child that young."

"Oh, dear God," Christine whispered.

Raoul trusted this doctor with all he had. On more than one occasion the man had stitched up a member of his family. For the first time, however, Raoul wanted to shove the doctor's words back into his mouth and force him to say something different.

"You can't come out here and tell us that!" Philippe's outburst ripped the hall in two and jerked Raoul's attention his way. He didn't blame the boy. Raoul was thinking exactly the same. "You have to fix this! I can't be without my sister!"

Shoulder's heaving and a face blood-red the boy's anger rounded his hand into a fist. Before it could collide with bone-crushing force to the wall behind him, Raoul lurched. His hands landed like a rock on Philippe's shoulder forcing him firmly, but carefully, back down to his seat.

"Is it possible for a heart to change rhythm?"

Raoul looked up from Philippe's panting as Erik's voice floated woefully from the window. He'd spent the last few hours staring at Paris as if contemplating the world's ultimate betrayal against him. Night deepened, making the only thing staring back into the room being the reflection of his yellow eyes. Ordinarily it would have chilled Raoul to the marrow, but instead, he saw in them that same searching pilgrim.

"A heart can love, wilt, hate, but can it change the way it beats?" Erik finally turned.

Raoul swore he saw unshed tears glistening behind those very human eyes. They didn't seem so monstrous to him now. The thought could have unmanned him if Raoul didn't practice keeping himself in check.

"Is it possible for love to truly be like music? So flawless in its beauty that if you displace one note the entire piece diminishes? So strong that a father would rather die than see his children suffer?" Erik was still as he stood there. "Somebody tell me. I never had a father's love. I never heard such music."

Out of the corner of his eyes, Raoul noted how André had looked up. Raoul met Erik's eyes and shared a tormented gaze with him. It forced his hand, still resting on Philippe's slowly rising and falling shoulders to tighten. Erik eyed Anna intently as he spoke directly to her.

"When Simone was born, I knew what I had passed to her, and I wanted to die. I wanted *her* to die with me. Does such make me a bad father?" Erik leveled attention on Raoul. "Because I took it back. I repented and took it back."

Raoul for once had no desire to shy away from the intensity of Erik's gaze. He tried to stammer a reply, but what answers did he have? Erik turned to Anna again.

"Her eyes never reflected anything but the wonder of a child. Anna?" Erik choked. "I need her back."

Raoul's soul withered. He remembered the agony of his own daughter's death as if it were as fresh as the coming dawn.

"I need my little girl," Erik begged taking two heavy steps toward the doctor. "There is something in her that is different. I cannot hear the music without her. My son cannot mature without her. They complete each other." He glanced at Philippe and curled his arms around himself as if trying to hug open air. "I cannot feel *anything*. Someone make me feel *something* because feeling nothing hurts."

Raoul heard himself swallow and wondered if the rest did. In the years he shared his life entwined with Erik's, he never once saw a man behind the monster. Anna stood. Thank God. Erik looked so large and vulnerable; Raoul didn't know what to do. She reached up with a quivering hand and removed Erik's mask. Raoul swallowed again. For the first time he could recall, that savage face didn't repulse him but held him transfixed. He didn't trust the feeling. Raoul watched as she dried the tears on his mangled cheeks as Erik looked down at her. Standing there,

Raoul felt like an intruder.

"I see her in you," Erik whispered. "How will I be able to keep on if I see her in you?"

"I know, Erik." She wiped a tear from his golden eye. "I see her in you too."

"She has to grow up, so she can tell you our secret. She promised me she would tell you what it is like. She promised."

Raoul let go of Philippe's shoulder suddenly feeling too close to Erik and Anna's intimacy. He felt Christine's hand brush his, but he walked out of her reach. He didn't want to be touched right now. Not physically. Not emotionally.

"What secret?" Anna asked through a clogged throat. "What promise?"

Erik rested his forehead against hers and grabbed the back of her neck. "She promised she would tell you what it is like for a daughter to be adored by her father; for a daughter to be so completely and utterly loved by her father."

Raoul cursed as Anna's tears shook her body. She collapsed into Erik's arms. Raoul had never felt so helpless in all his days.

It's the children who always show the adults the stark reality of their mistakes.

"Go," Anna sniffled, gently pushing Erik to the doctor. "She needs you to sing to her." All watched as Erik, and the physician slipped away, and door swished shut behind them.

"Mademoiselle Barret," Raoul whispered when he finally found his voice. His was dragging lead as he walked toward her. "I cannot find the words to say how profoundly sorry I am for—"

Anna's slap smacked the words right off his mouth. Tears poured out her accusing eyes and instead of reacting, Raoul stepped off and back into place.

"Not now, Monsieur le Comte," she hissed. "Not. Now."

EIGHTEEN

Simone should be outside playing for the chickens and spinning like a fool in mad circles, free from the confines of anything but her spirit. Instead, beds that ran the length of both sides of the room flanked her. Fabric partitions protected some beds, but not hers. She lay there exposed, vulnerable, and smaller than Philippe had ever seen her.

Arms folded, weight distributed evenly on both feet, and his chest puffed out, Philippe stood guard over her bedside. A dull ache wound behind his lower back. He could move, but he refused. Standing there like a fortress made him feel impenetrable. It took all his effort to tear his mother away from Simone's side so she could get some rest under the Persian's care. Someone had to. Hours had passed, and his father was nowhere to be found—a thought that made Philippe stiffen. Philippe had come to learn that his father had a habit of bolting away and hiding—at least when it came to Paris.

A nun shuffled by. He nodded politely at her yet had the sense her expression was more pity for Simone than empathy. He waited until she was gone to dig his thumb and forefinger against his eyes. He tried to pluck the sleep from them, but that was as impossible as trying to rid himself of the image of Simone getting shot.

"Monsieur?"

Philippe drew his hand down his face. His fingers stopped at his chin before he lifted it to the ceiling. His hand turned to a rock-hard fist. He scrubbed his mouth with the back of it and did his best to keep his fragile patience in check.

"Monsieur le Vicomte." He cleared his throat but didn't turn as the vicomte approached the bedside.

"I told you. I go against convention. You may call me André."

"You hardly acted against convention when I came calling yesterday."

"That was yesterday." He laid something on the foot of the bed. "Your sister's violin. I hope you don't mind that I have it. I procured a case for it."

Philippe's eyes narrowed. Was that some peace offering? He had to force his fist not to return to his mouth. The violin seemed to be dying too.

"Even a stranger could see your sister was... is attached to it. Can I get you anything? Perhaps you're hungry, or in need of a drink?" He gestured down the ward. "I can take you anywhere you want—"

"I'm not leaving this bedside."

The vicomte—pardon, *André*—could take his guilt and ram it up his ass. Philippe cocked his neck side-to-side not use to having such thoughts.

"Has there been any change?" André asked.

What do you care? Philippe widened his legs and tightened his arms across his chest. "None. The doctors come and go, but there's no change. If I could, I would remove her from this abysmal place entirely. Take her someplace else to rest and hold her until..." Philippe looked away from his sister feeling his helplessness and regretting lowering his guard. He snapped his head back to André. "Why are you here? Our families are at war."

André didn't remove his eyes from Simone unlike everyone else that had passed by. Its pallor made her face look more skull-like, but the nobleman didn't react like when he first saw her. Hours ago he had wanted to charge Philippe down like an angry bull, and now he stared in compassion upon Simone.

Philippe didn't trust it.

"That may be true," André replied. "Although I may be my father's son, does that make me like him? You certainly are different from yours."

Grinding his teeth made Philippe's jaw tighten again. He eyed André suspiciously. "You needn't be cordial to me in light of my sister. I know I am the son of the Phantom."

André looked up from Simone and matched Philippe stance-for-stance. "Right now you are a man standing vigil over his sister's bedside; a noble and honorable act. Can we lose the pretenses and allow that to be the case?"

Philippe looked at him warily out of the corner of his eye.

"If you're anything like me," André continued carefully but sternly, "then your life has been an intricate web of half-truths. I don't pretend to know all the details that brought us here. Only that *my* parents were hunting *yours* and you are the namesake of an uncle I adore but never met. My parents perpetrated this. Not me. I thank you for not judging me by their tangled obsessions for one another."

His words forced Philippe heavily down on the stool beside the bed. It thumped back on two legs sending a boom throughout the ward. The place soon was as silent as before. He pressed his forearms to his thighs and stared at the violin. "Thank you for retrieving that."

Philippe looked up long enough to see André nod as he studied the shallow rise and fall of Simone's chest.

"This wasn't supposed to happen," the vicomte quietly murmured.

"I don't think any of this was supposed to happen." Philippe chewed back his sarcasm.

"What do you understand of it—Philippe?"

Philippe stared at his sister, his brows knitting together a history he didn't create. For once someone was standing across from him who was an equal of sorts. Philippe never could live up to the genius of his father, nor understand the sensitive mind behind the madman. He was too brilliant himself to be one with vagabonds, and too exuberant to be satisfied with monks.

Though he and André were as different as fox and hound, they had matured in the same chase. What *did* he understand of it?

Too tired to fight his thoughts any longer, Philippe took the imaginary olive branch. "Nothing, frankly. Nothing beyond I am Philippe Georges Marie, and this is my sister." His arm was heavy when he indicated Simone. "I live my life trying to understand the past that tangles my name to yours, and do so loved by the man your family hates—the man who loves us in the way he knows how, and who loves my mother more than life. That much I understand. That's worth something in all this."

"You speak highly of love, then. My father worships my mother, but she…" André's voice dipped. It made Philippe's brow twist in another way as he felt a pang of pity. "Do you understand him, your father, I mean? I often don't understand mine."

Philippe relaxed and shifted in his seat. He shrugged. "Sometimes. It's the world that doesn't understand him, and sadly they may now never understand Simone." He reached for the violin case and removed the instrument. He reverently tucked it to her chest and wrapped her frail arms around it as if it would be some magic cure that turned back time.

"I don't think my parents understand him." André was somber. "But I would if you enlighten me."

Philippe looked up. André's fingertips rested on the bed, and he looked at Simone as if he desired to sweep way the flaxen curl hanging between her eyes. The past was still too raw for such a tentative display of friendship. Philippe reached forward stroked the hair out of her face.

"André, to understand them, is to understand music…"

As the boys continued to speak, Christine's hand slid dejectedly down a fabric partition two beds away. Safely out of their sight she eavesdropped on a tale of the Angel of Music unlike any she had ever heard. Years of grief flowed silently down her cheeks as Philippe shared stories about Erik and Anna, and told them through the admiring eyes of a child. He unraveled a tale of their life beyond the uncertainty of a manhunt. One that was fed by a mutual love language, something Christine longed to own with Raoul but didn't possess. Even though the partition kept her securely out of view, she felt exposed, like a sinner suddenly pointed out in a crowd. As long as she breathed she would never forget André's uncompleted sentence: *My father worships my mother, but she...*

Christine tried not to visit the truth that was feasting on her heart; that she'd shut her husband out pursuing the love of another man, and neglected a love that was devoted, kind, and unconditional. Christine's silent confession soaked her chin in tears. The river was a long time in the making.

Hearing her son ask careful questions of his tentative new friend and listening to Philippe ask his own in reply, painted a picture of what time had done to the young lives that never asked to be shaped in such a way. The corrosive guilt of it all eroded her from the inside out. Christine backed away from the conversation knowing she could never have Erik, and that she would never love him the same again. His soul belonged to another, and it was not Anna.

It belonged to Simone.

NINETEEN

Bright morning sun bathe the Tuileries. The garden was alive with couples. The city of lights loved as usual while Erik's heart beat wooden in his chest. Row after row of roses burst into full bloom along a hedgerow sending their heady fragrance floating through the morning air.

Erik dragged his hand along the blossoms, caressing them as he aimlessly roamed. He paused now and then; ignoring the heads he turned, to select the most perfect, unblemished roses he could. Last time he wandered this garden he kept to shadows like a demented stalker. He cared less who looked on him now or how this manhunt ultimately ended. The only care he had in the world lay in a bed that swallowed her whole.

Erik gently reached to a rose. Its red petals folded in on one another, not totally asleep yet not entirely awake, much like Simone. Erik snapped the stem. Dew splattered on his wrist. He lifted the rose to the false nose on his mask and tried desperately not to feel the sucking pain in his chest.

"The Persian suspected you might be here, if not at the opera house."

Erik lowered the rose as that voice shredded his brain. The great and noble Raoul came seeking him, instead of hunting him?

Erik lifted his eyes from the delicate flower and pinned them on the approaching comte. Raoul paused only long enough to wave off the police that accompanied him. Erik watched as they fell backward and allowed the comte to stride forward alone. So Raoul would not shrink in the presence of the Phantom any longer? Was Erik supposed to be impressed? He addressed the rose.

"It takes my daughter's blood for you to call off your hounds?"

"The escort is Legard's doing," Raoul said. Erik flicked his eyes back toward the small crowd of officers, and sure enough, Legard stood in their center. "You're not exactly in your right mind, leaving your child and coming out in public like this. People have been wondering where you are."

The folds of the rose were soft beneath Erik's fingers. Should he remove the thorns or would it be best for Simone to know that things of beauty often come with their ugly side as well? He addressed Raoul's audacity to judge him. "I don't care about the public and why would I not be in my right mind, Monsieur?" *Leave the thorns*, he thought. Erik walked the hedgerow ignoring Raoul's footfalls behind him.

"There are people worried about you. It would help if you returned to the hospital."

Erik stopped, causing Raoul to stop with him. When he began walking again so did his newfound shadow. There was a hint of concern to Raoul's voice that sickened Erik's stomach. "No, it is not time. When she wakes, she will need a bouquet, a perfect one, for a perfect little girl." He scrutinized another rose ignoring the extended cast of Raoul's shadow as it fell in front of him.

"It *is* the time, Erik. You can't be out here wandering—"

Erik raised his hand and cut him off. A white rose perhaps? No, the yellow ones to match her eyes. "Who tends these gardens?"

"I have no idea." Now there was a hint of exasperation to Raoul's voice. Typical.

"They need to plant more yellow." Erik turned and trained his yellow eyes on his nemesis. "So that a thousand golden eyes can stare at you every time you come out here. Why *did* you come looking for me? Could you not send the Persian or the good Inspector? Or do you suddenly feel guilty and this act is some noble gesture to make you feel useful? Or perchance you come here to arrest me lest you think I am still obsessed with your wife and I am suddenly going to turn my heart over to her. I assure you the games between us ended long ago."

Raoul shifted, glanced back toward Legard, and shifted again. His little box step betrayed his nerves.

"You need to return to the hospital. Mademoiselle Barret is asking for you, as is your son. I have a carriage waiting." He gestured to Erik's clothing. "And the Persian thought to send a fresh shirt."

The crimson color of Simone's blood had faded to a murky brown. Erik pawed at it, rubbing it against his chest as if trying to get her blood to flow directly into his heart. "No. I need a part of her close."

"Change. It's unnerving to see."

A shaking rage lifted to the surface blasting away Erik's vulnerability. "It unnerves you? Let it unnerve you, you noble son-of-a-bitch!" Clouds shredded with his cry.

Rifles cocked. The comte gestured immediately, halting the Inspector's approach.

"No," Erik huffed, his knifelike glare honing in on Raoul. "Let them come. Let them shoot. *Let them kill me.* I should have died as intended and never permitted your brother into my life!" Raw anguish ripped apart the remnants of the clouds. Raoul's brows raced up in response and his stance hardened. "You know so little of, Erik! Fear *that*, Monsieur le Comte! Forget your wife and fear my history with the great Philippe de Chagny! If not for me listening to his lessons on compassion and redemption I would be dead, and my daughter would *never* have been born, and she would not be dying right now!"

"What rot are you speaking?"

"The rot I speak matters not when my daughter is dying, you nefarious fool!"

"This was an accident! A horrible tragedy—"

"That is right," Erik jerked his head in the direction Raoul looked. "Check and see how far away your guards are because Erik is unpredictable again." He clutched his roses and swaggered down the length of the hedgerow toward Raoul. "Now, why would that be? Could poor unhappy Erik be that vengeful menace The Phantom right now because of the sins that are finally *yours*?" He stopped in front of Raoul and looked him up and down. "Where is it? Where is your silver platter, so that I can hand you my life on it? That is what you still what? Even though I let you go. I gave you Christine. I gave up my obsession with you. I gave you your life so many times I have lost count. I have never *wanted* to kill before; I did so because I had to. But I feel it in my marrow now. I want to kill *you*." Erik's head shot toward the sound of boots as the police marched forward. He pointed toward them. "But yet again you win because doing that will do nothing to ease my pain. So I stand here and try to decipher why you—of all people—came looking for me, but I have none. Finally, *pity* is not in the Phantom's vocabulary. The only one who deserves such my daughter."

He pointed a shaking finger under Raoul's chin. His hand snaked up the length of his face. Like a boney spider's web, his skeletal fingers covered Raoul's expression. The comte instinctively turned his head, bringing Erik's hand with him.

"It may have been Loup's bullet," Erik hissed, inches from Raoul's ear. "It may have been Legard's, but regardless *your manhunt* pulled the trigger. Hand at the level of your eyes, Monsieur."

Erik shoved Raoul's face away and snapped his cloak; the sound it made ricocheted against the air. He knocked Raoul aside with his shoulder as he barreled down the hedgerow, pleased that a mask kept the tears of a father glistening privately in his eyes. He was more than willing for the world to see his wrath right now, but not his anguish.

Being a Phantom was far easier than being human.

TWENTY

The doctors made their rounds every hour like clockwork. They passed the rows of beds; their heads occasionally tipped together in some private conversation. Anna felt their eyes upon her each time they passed. Doctors must know the scene of a mother's vigil by heart, so why did they have to pause to stare at her each time they walked by? Anna laid her head down against Simone's bedside again careful not to disturb her or the violin she held.

Sweet boy that André. He'd managed to achieve making Anna feel something other than agony in the last few hours be it through the violin he returned or the blanket he brought her before Philippe, and he had roamed off.

Anna pulled the blanket further up her lap as her lip trembled. Simone needed to wake up. Just wake, and play, and say things that make no sense, that way this all could be some strange dream. A tear slipped out of Anna's eye, as she knew her silent pleas were nothing more than wishful thoughts. Simone just lay quietly in that bed never knowing the tears her mother shed. Blinded by grief, Anna never saw the cup that appeared on the bedside table beside her until a voice turned her attention to it

"It's hot tea," the voice said softly.

Anna lifted her head and looked over her shoulder. The

comtesse stood behind her, her eyes cast down and to the side.
"My husband went in search of Erik this morning," she
continued. "The Persian is keeping company with our sons."

Anna turned away and draped her arm across Simone's waist,
refusing to give the comtesse a second look. "Vahid. His name
is Vahid."

The comtesse fidgeted, Anna could tell. She heard the swish
of her skirts and click of her boots on the floor.

"I wasn't aware of his name," the comtesse said.

Of course, you weren't. Anna heard unease to the comtesse's
voice. She wanted to take her fancy teacup, shove it back into
her hands and tell her to go away. The comtesse was making the
air around her precious child colder than it should be.

"I can bring the entire pot if you'd like."

Unbelievable. Anna wanted *precisely* that right now. An
entire cup of the comtesse's forced-brewed grief. Anna looked
up but didn't turn around.

"You can't have Erik, you know. Not in the way you wish
him." She heard the swish and shuffle behind her again, this time
even more agitated than before. "All these years and you've not
wanted what you have but wanted what can't have. Do you
remember when you first held your son?" Anna asked abruptly
half looking over her shoulder.

"What mother doesn't?"

"Erik delivered Philippe. He was ecstatic he arrived and so
happy that he was perfect. He loves that boy so much." Anna
couldn't stand the seconds not looking at Simone, so she looked
back on her daughter again. She covered her lips with the back
of her hand as soon as she heard Simone struggle for a breath. It
pressed the salt of her tears against her mouth and muffled her
words. "Have you ever seen Erik happy?"

The silence behind her spoke enough.

Anna lowered her hand and raised her voice. "I saw him
happy when Philippe was born. But when we had Simone, I saw
a joy in his eyes that could only have been yanked down from
heaven. When did you ever see him that way?"

Anna finally turned around. She had to know if all the

shuffling going on behind her was for reason of nerves or guilt. The comtesse kept her gaze downcast and didn't reply. Somehow Anna didn't expect her to.

"This is so utterly unnecessary." Hot tears marred Anna's voice. "One confession by you may have put it this manhunt to rest years ago. I have done *nothing* to you. I beg of you, give that man one moment of peace and end this manhunt the *right* way before our daughter—and his joy—goes to God."

Anna gathered the blanket from her lap and shoved herself to her feet, feeling choked by the pain of potentially never holding Simone again. Only one person could stem her agony. She pushed the blanket against the comtesse's breast.

"If you will excuse me, I need Erik." Anna bolted past her but stopped and turned back. "I don't want your tea. I want you, for once, not to think of yourself."

⇒•••————•••————••⇐

The confrontation in the Tuileries followed Raoul back to the hospital as if it were chained to his leg. Erik's threats didn't frighten him. His humanity did. It was hard to discern if Erik was still a madman. Why did Raoul even wonder such? He rubbed the back of his neck as he walked the hospital halls. He must be tired, that's why he wasn't thinking clearly.

"Good Morning, *Père.*"

Raoul stopped short, nearly plowing headfirst into his son and Philippe. Raoul scowled as Philippe's expression socked him right in the gut. The boy looked like he had aged ten years in a single night. Raoul nodded to his son but addressed Erik's.

"Has your father returned yet? He refused to ride back in the carriage."

The boy shook his head. "Not yet, but I appreciate you going to look for him. I suppose everyone handles shock in their own way." Truer words Raoul hadn't heard in a long while. It realigned the way Raoul had judged Erik's early morning stroll. "Monsieur le Comte, I—"

Raoul lifted a brow when Philippe abruptly stopped and

looked to André. His son nodded encouragingly. One would have to have been blind not to see the tentative alliance budding between the two. It always was children who could so easily make amends. Raoul gestured encouragingly to Philippe. "Go on." "Do you wish me to ask?" André offered.

Philippe shook his head. "No. She is my sister." He stepped forward. "I know what I represent to you, Monsieur le Comte. I'm the son of a man you despise. I ask you to set that aside. My father's history is not mine. I'm not him, and he would never think to do this, but I want to… that is I would like to take my sister and—"

Philippe faltered. Raoul watched the boy struggle to be a man as he scrubbed his eyes on his shirtsleeve. André squeezed Philippe's shoulder, shook it, and took over.

"Philippe and I have been speaking. He's been telling me about Simone," André explained. Raoul gave an abbreviated nod more so to settle it into his mind how easily André seemed to have connected with this little girl, then to acknowledge his son. "If the doctors can do no more for her here other than monitor her, he wants to bring her to a quiet place to rest."

Raoul felt a sharp pain in his chest. "Have they said they could no longer help her?"

"They can only keep her comfortable," Philippe blurted, finding his voice. Raoul felt the heaviness of the implication of his words. "She's different. She is not used to places like this. Simone is used to the countryside, to quiet places. Should she wake here, it will frighten her." Philippe's voice cracked enough for André to step in.

"Respectfully, *Père*, can we move her to Chagny?"

That blasted away Raoul's exhaustion. His son had gone mad! "Absolutely not! I hear all the young man says, André, but—"

"You have the power and authority to take any number of physicians with you, and it won't be the first time you've done something like that. Our physicians can tend her there until God decides whether she will live or—"

"Please, André, don't say it," Philippe whispered. "It's alright. He doesn't approve, leave it be. I don't want to make anything worse."

André stopped when Philippe bowed his head and looked

away. It didn't make Raoul's decision any more comfortable.

"André," Raoul chose his words carefully as he took his son by the arm and moved him away from Philippe. "To move that child is to move her family with her, and I will not have Chagny disgraced by—"

"Your prejudices and obsessions?"

André yanked his arm free and boldly moved back to where he was. He stood sideways between his father and Philippe. "We are not a disgrace, *Père*, for we have nothing to do with your history with the Phantom." André gestured between him and Philippe. "Your hostilities are perpetuated because you've not stopped once to let go of them. Chagny will be mine one day, and I will govern it by the family creed that you seem to ignore."

"Vicomte, not now!"

"Yes now." André pushed back. "Do you remember that creed, *Père*? Fidelity and compassion: the sacred endowments of our mind. Where did *your* compassion go?" André pointed back to the ward. "There is a little girl in there dying—"

"André," Philippe whispered.

"No, I won't remain silent no matter how harsh the reality, Philippe. You want this for her, and you will have it if only my father would see we no longer deserve to shoulder a past we didn't create. If they want to live perpetuating their hatred, then let them. But I am Chagny as much as he is Chagny and the stigmas that are his are not mine. I was able to find my compassion. The question is—can my father?"

Raoul had compassion, but he chose to bury it below Erik's threats on his life, a detail his son didn't know. While he understood the reasoning behind the request, the idea of Erik on the grounds of Chagny didn't sit well. It was downright unnerving. Erik was as unpredictable as he'd ever been, likely grief-driven into being more so. André's request would put all of Chagny at risk. However, when his son faced him, Raoul wasn't looking at a boy anymore. He was looking at a man capable of holding the reigns of Chagny far better than he ever did. A man he'd been blind to.

"Please, *Père*," André urged. "He's my friend."

"And his parents are wanted criminals. Son," Raoul put a hand on André's shoulder, but his attempt at solidarity didn't register on the boy's face. "There is far more to this than meets the eye. I have the safety of your mother to consider, and even if I brought a legion of guards with us, there are certain places where the past should never intersect."

"You mean at Chagny?" André flipped Raoul's hand from his shoulder. "What if was Evangeline?"

"What?"

"The bullet. What if it hit Evangeline and she was dying in that room now. Wouldn't you move the sun and earth not to see her suffer?"

The implication hit Raoul between the eyes and nearly blinded him. He'd been trying since the moment that bullet rang out not to picture his daughter at Simone's age. He'd been desperately trying to bury any form of empathy from his own daughter's death. That was growing harder to do by the second.

"Father!"

Philippe's sudden announcement saved Raoul from having to answer but didn't spare him a heaping serving of remorse as soon as he looked down the hall. The roses Erik clutched were bent in two as he walked; a clear sign of a disturbed mind. Nuns and doctors dodged out of his way, but it seemed Erik didn't even notice. He walked like a man not sure of his footsteps. Raoul knew that dejected walk. He'd moved in that same hopeless manner after laying his daughter in her cradle for very last time. Raoul didn't betray what he was thinking but watched Erik's approach with a furrow in his brow. Erik stopped at Philippe's side.

"You came back," Philippe said, the surprise to his voice flipping Raoul's heart sideways. "Flowers?"

Seeming startled, Erik looked down at his fist and the once perfect roses that lay blemished in his hand. "For Simone," he replied distantly. "For when she—"

"Will you answer a question, Erik, without me needing to keep my hand at the level of my eyes?" Raoul suddenly snapped, unable to bear Erik's pain any longer.

Raoul's voice was like a dagger into Erik's ear. As soon as he had entered the hospital, he had tunnel vision on reaching Anna and his son. It seemed at every turn Raoul would be there, blocking his way. Erik swallowed a growl.

"And what question is that, Monsieur?"

"Why did you name your son after my brother?"

The noise in Erik's head became blaringly loud. Now, was not the time for the comte's sudden interest in history. "Why?"

"I have a decision to make, and I must know."

Erik looked at Philippe and the questions now on the rise. "It repulses me that at this particular time of my family's grief you choose to indulge in your need for closure," Erik spat, not entirely sure how much information he was willing to give. If not for Philippe's expression, Erik would have walked pointedly down the hall. "You and your brother were night and day. He was as irreproachable in conscience and compassion to me as you are in your lack of them. Oh, the irony that each of you would hold a pillar in my particular part of hell."

"Get to your point." Raoul urged. "Time is of the essence."

Erik didn't appreciate Raoul's mention of time, not when his daughter's life was in the balance. "I named my son after him to remind myself that there is such power as compassion, and in that, forgiveness." He laid a hand on Philippe's arm and turned the boy down the hall at first determined to leave Raoul puzzling through that comment. He couldn't, however, and jerked his attention backward. "I can love or does my madness constantly cloak that imagery for you? What man would not be driven to such thought as murder because of what has happened due to your hunt? Do you think for one moment I *actually* would kill you and make good on my threats or that I would make your life a priority over my daughter's? Leave off, Monsieur le Comte. Let my threats be just that; words spoken in grief and anger." Raoul stood unflinchingly at his vicomte's side. It was as if the man had gone numb. Erik took advantage of his frozen stance to lean into his outrage. "Your decisions can go to hell. I have made them for you. Lock me away. Throw me in prison. Send me to my death if you will, but for now, let me be like anybody else to chart my way through this part of hell like a normal man."

TWENTY-ONE

The townhome swallowed her. It had been for days. The halls seemed to pulse with conviction with each step Christine took toward her husband's library. Raoul had wrestled with taking his family and leaving the hospital, and it took a lot of soul-searching to realize he did so out of respect. Hovering over Erik and his family seemed wrong; especially since Raoul had confessed to Christine that it was his fault, a child lay dying. That confession stuck awkwardly in her ear, knowing the role she played in it from the start. Raoul had turned into a broken man over the last few days; not since Philippe's death has Christine seen him so burdened. The family pride had gone out of his eyes.

Christine laid a hand on the library door but paused before opening it. She'd spent the last few days insisting on solitude as she tried to figure out the condition of her heart. The last image she had of Erik hovering over a child's bedside had burned a hole in her heart, and Anna's words battered Christine day and night. Her guilt was a fever ever turning her in fits that nothing could relieve. Obsessing over her shamefulness had finally come to a head, and she could no longer bear to bury it any longer. The breath she took was shaky as she opened the library door.

André looked up at her as soon as she entered. Christine

smiled weakly at him, noting with a sick sort of irony the copy of *Macbeth* he held. She glanced across the room toward Raoul as he paced in front of the windows. Her choices had impacted both of these men over the years. It fitted that they were both there to hear her try to set their history right.

"Raoul, may we speak?" she asked quietly, causing her husband to stop and look up.

"I'll leave," André said moving to rise.

"No stay," Christine said. If she was going to wash her conscious, she had to do so before both of them.

Raoul rubbed his temple as he walked. Christine felt his sigh. "I don't know how much longer I can sit in this townhome," Raoul murmured. "Leaving Legard standing watch over Erik makes me feel like a bloody mongrel. The hospital just sent word. The child isn't improving. No matter what I do, I keep seeing the bullet tear through her leaving her on the floor like a flightless bird." He pivoted in the same spot as a moment ago and switched directions. "Never did I think I would ever empathize with a madman. I have known nothing of Erik beyond the monster he is, but now I see him as a father and, God help me, the two images are rioting within me."

"There has been no change with the child?" Christine echoed.

"No, and I'm responsible."

His statement knifed her. "You're not responsible, Raoul. I am."

"Christine—"

"No, Raoul, it is time I spoke."

Only on stage did Christine's voice find such passion, but this wasn't an opera. Something foreboding surrounded Raoul making Christine flutter like a lost butterfly.

"How can I possibly make you both understand?" She couldn't, that was the reason why this was so painful. It would be best that she just spoke and didn't think. "I yearned for Erik's guidance and became seduced with the illusion of the Angel of Music through the years. But in all this, I realized he was nothing more than a man too."

Raoul placed his hands on his hips. "I know all this, Christine."

"You know nothing of it!" Her shout even surprised herself. "I rejected *a man* due to my immaturity."

Raoul had gone silent for longer than necessary. He wasn't pleased. "Christine, don't torture yourself over this. The reasons why we see him in a different light is my burden." He came to her side and lifted her chin, forcing her to meet his eyes. "You rejected a manipulative *madman*. You only assumed that you loved and sympathized with him as a defensive way to protect yourself. What has happened doesn't eliminate what he put you through. I sympathize with him for I lost a daughter I love. I'm torn inside because I identify with him in this. I long to make amends to that little girl, but I can't let go of what he did to you. Not now, not ever."

"He is mad because of me!"

"Christine. You're not responsible for that man's madness."

"No, I am responsible for all of this because of how deeply I love him."

Raoul stepped off from her. "You... what?"

"Loup spoke the truth. I love Erik. I always have."

The room had gone strangely cold. Even André's expression made the air tingle. Raoul thought to dismiss him, but the young man revealed to him in the hospital deserved to stay. Raoul's hands landed on his hips again, this time to block the absurdity of her confession. But it wasn't absurd. He knew. It leached out in the way she paced. It screamed in her voice. Her confession was a rotated puzzle piece sliding perfectly into place. Raoul fought the tension in his jaw to allow her to speak, for if he opened his mouth right now, he didn't trust what he would say.

"My jealousy perpetuated this entire manhunt," she rambled. "I never confessed years ago because so long as you vowed to protect me from Erik, it meant you were looking for him, and there was still a chance for me to win his love."

Raoul's tension moved from his jaw to his voice. "Confessed, what?"

What he heard next throughout Christine's halted and awkward admissions, from Erik saving her life from Richard Barret to the blackmail by Loup, and the arrangement she made with him to keep Erik out of his reach, turned Raoul's world upside down.

"All these years I have wanted you both," Christine wailed, tearfully. "I've been a jealous, selfish fool! I still have my child, and he may very well lose his, and dear God when I think of losing my family. Teach me how to love my family the *right* way, Raoul. In the way Erik has come to love Anna and his son, and his…dear God, Raoul, she is only a little girl! *What have I done?*"

As Christine collapsed into his arms, sobs shaking her entire body, Raoul had to force his arms to curl around her. Teach her to love in the way Erik has come to love Anna? What of the years that *he* had loved her? With one sentence Christine had succeeded in draining the fight from Raoul's body. Looking around, he searched the library for his sanity. All he found was his son slapping a copy of *Macbeth* down on the armchair seconds before he bolted from the room.

⁂

Raoul's heartbreak-heavy footsteps echoed down the hall.

The sun was lowering outside, and his hours-long walk had done nothing to rip his mind free of depressive thoughts. Ordinarily, he would have come home and checked on Christine, but this time he bypassed the idea, surprised at how easy it was in light of his feelings. Head down and thoughts heavy, he entered his library and closed the door behind him. Immediately the room was too quiet. Ironic, considering the battleground it could have been earlier. The curtains were drawn shut and a new fire burned in the hearth. The maids had been here.

Raoul shucked his jacket and tossed it on the settee. He tugged his tie and let it hang loosely around his neck. He leaned on the mantel and stared numbly into the flames surprised at how cold his palms were compared to hot his knees grew. He was so absorbed in the heat and the flicker of mind-dulling flames that he almost didn't see the book sliding across the mantle toward him.

Raoul blinked and shook his head clear. His son had appeared beside him.

Dieu. André. What must the boy be thinking in light of all this? Raoul stared at the book noting how the thought made life seem even weightier.

"I think you should read that," André said, his voice decisive.

Raoul picked the book up, choosing not to address his son's inappropriate tone. The leather on the spine was cracked as if the book had been open and closed a hundred times or more. The cover curled slightly backward on itself wafting out the smell of old ink.

"Why? What is it?"

"Uncle Philippe's private journal."

Raoul wasn't prepared for that answer. His eyes slid from the worn cover to his son. André's stance was firm and unmoved by the look his father shot him. Raoul was too tired to unravel the moment.

"Where did you—"

"Get it? From a hidden drawer in the bookcase in his chambers. I discovered and broke into it *years* ago—I think I was twelve—but I never had the guts to read it once I realized what it was. I had too much respect for you and Chagny to breach his privacy. Safe to say that respect has gone out the window."

Well, that answered Raoul's question of what André may have been feeling. His son shoved off the mantel.

"Read it," he snapped. Raoul noted the authoritative clip to his voice that betrayed his sixteen years. Chagny will have a formidable leader when the victomte's time came. "Read it and then end this manhunt. I think what you'll learn will change the course of everything you thought you knew about your so-called madman. I suggest you start on the page I marked. The page about a man known only as The Shade." Raoul felt André's sigh vibrate against his chest. "Reading it has managed to make me gain more respect for my uncle than I ever had, and less respect for what you have allowed to become of Chagny."

Raoul didn't acknowledge that his son had strode out of the room, leaving behind boulder-sized words. He could barely accept that he held a piece of his brother that he never knew existed. Sliding a thumb and finger between the pages separated by a bookmark, he eased the journal open.

By the time he finished reading, the fire had grown dim, and Raoul had discovered what it truly meant to be Comte de Chagny.

TWENTY-TWO

Fat raindrops rolled down the window distorting everything outside. If Simone were awake, she'd liken the sound of the clapping rain to marbles hitting a tile floor. The sound would be pink and fuchsia. They'd probably taste like something ridiculous: beets or an underdone potato.

"She'd say they'd taste like strudel," Anna muttered.

Erik turned away from the window, a ghost of a smile on his lips. He was unaware he'd been thinking aloud. One glance at Anna as she curled on the chair next to Simone's bedside, made Erik's chest grow tighter than he thought it could. Deeper lines had etched in the corner of her eyes over the last few days making the hard life already worn into her face grow harder. If it were possible for Erik's mask to change with his expressions, it would show every trial as well.

Philippe busied himself with pacing up and down the now empty ward. Empty at least of patients. Marksmen flanked the far door, their hawk-like eyes watching Erik's every move. He'd come to ignore them. The life he associated with a manhunt didn't matter any longer—the only life that did lay in the bed. The last news was not good. The child was fading, and little more could be done but wait until…

Erik couldn't think of it.

He tried hard not to think of anything when the door opened and three people he wanted least to see walked down the ward. Philippe stopped pacing at the sight of the vicomte, yet Raoul and Christine made Erik restless. Legard had followed them in next. Erik folded his arms and stood at the foot of Simone's bed blocking his family from any more of their unrelenting persecution. Could they not leave until the inevitable happened?

"I will not be removed from this spot, Monsieur le Comte." Try to take him now despite his surrender and Erik would mow every one of them down before they uttered a second breath.

"I'm not." Raoul stopped a respectable distance from Simone's bedside and gestured for his wife to move forward. The change in demeanor between them was thick in the room. "The comtesse has something to say."

Anna shifted in her spot. It was the most she had moved in days. Erik watched as she stared Christine down when she came into view. Erik looked away from Anna to study the tears in Christine's eyes. Her voice shook drastically.

"This... this is killing you."

Erik arched a brow Christine couldn't see. It matched the huff that hopped out of Anna's mouth. Killing him? Erik died inside the moment that bullet hit his daughter. His response was to look at Raoul's unmoved expression just as Christine did. It was apparent any support she sought wouldn't come from Raoul. He gestured with the book again like a father encouraging a reprimanded child to do something unpleasant.

Christine's swallow was audible. "I mean to say, that you'd die of a broken heart if not able to love that little girl, wouldn't you? You surrender and sacrifice your life so she could live without this manhunt."

If she lived. Erik looked at Anna. She was holding back tears but fighting hard not to let anyone know. He could tell by the way her nose reddened. Erik turned back to Christine. "I had said as much about dying of a broken heart years ago when you left me, Christine," he admitted evenly, knowing he could say anything in front of Anna. "But I have come to know a grander love than what I held for you. My family is greater than I am. I would sacrifice everything to spare them this madness. But it seems the madness has not spared them at all, now has it? Have you a point?" Erik felt the passing seconds as if a clock were lodged in his chest. If they weren't here to haul him away, then they needed to go. Simone needed him.

Christine inched forward as if not sure of her steps. He watched her look beyond him and nod to Anna as if some unspoken request was floating between them. Christine looked up and met his eyes.

"Forgive me. Please, Erik, forgive me."

As soon as the words leapt from her mouth, Christine's knees gave out. She sank to the floor and clutched the edge of his cloak.

"Please, forgive me for all I've done!" Christine looked up and searched around her. "I beg all of you for forgiveness for perpetuating this manhunt with my jealousy and selfish intent. Erik, you saved me years ago, and I never told anyone because I was jealous of her." Christine looked around him and met Anna's steadfast gaze. "I apologize and am so, so sorry. Forgive me, and I swear I will make amends… I will do anything. Anything!"

Anna sucked in a long breath when Christine shifted to stare up at Erik. She clung to his cloak even tighter desperately trying to hold on to one last scrap of him.

"This must end," Christine hoarsely whispered. "For the sake of that baby girl."

Erik had to wonder what she meant because her words indicated one thing yet her slavish position to him said another. "Christine." Erik's voice was incredibly gentle. He came to one knee before her and pried her grip from his cloak. She refused to let go, but Erik forced her. "Just let me live like anybody else."

"That is what my brother wanted for you," Raoul said. "In this."

Raoul took Christine's hand and drew her securely, but gently to his side giving Erik the freedom to move next to Anna. He extended a book.

Erik took it.

"Once I know this answer I pray to have the same strength as my brother once did." Raoul had taken a tone eerily similar to his brother's causing Erik to listen with interest. Raoul cleared his throat before moving on. Erik wondered what emotion he was shoving down. "The last several hours have revealed a history I never knew you had with my brother." He indicated the book Erik held. It seemed so much had piled upon Raoul's shoulders that it was a wonder he didn't fall. "I already believe I know the answer after reading what my brother had to say about you, but I need to hear from you. Swear upon the life of that little girl, answer truthfully, Erik. Did you kill my brother? You will not set foot in my chateau if you did, so help me God. I will burn alive before I let that innocent little girl down, but you will leave Chagny faster than words can fly if you so much do anything to harm my family."

"Leave Chagny?" Anna asked. Erik felt her reach for his forearm. He laid a hand on hers to keep her still. He wondered the reason for that statement too but questioned more the contents of the book.

"I did not," he replied. "This is his journal; I take it? He told me years ago he was keeping one regarding his escapades in my cellars—his escapades and those damn life lessons he was teaching me." Erik stroked the book. The words were no sooner out his mouth before Raoul flinched. "You just displayed the difference between you and your brother." Erik lifted the book slightly to emphasize his point. "He did not fear to know the truth about any circumstance, or the truth about me."

"The truth? I am forced to take you at your word on that for I fear I may never know the truth of anything anymore. But somehow my brother has made me believe you to be a man of integrity." A bewildered laugh jumped out of Raoul's mouth as he paused as if to let that idea sink in. When he glanced in the direction of Simone, he sobered. "I keep thinking of the daughter I lost because of this manhunt. Thinking of what Philippe would do and…" Raoul's nostrils flared, and his jaw tightened. He was holding something painful at bay. "I see you as a blasted father now, and I can't do this anymore. I can't pretend that you're not human to me." Arms akimbo he stared heavenward. Turning, he jabbed a finger in the air between them. "If my brother were here today to see how children have suffered..." The finger sliced the air. "This is over. I can't endure it anymore. I miss my baby girl, and I can't see another man suffer as I have. I will see to it you're not pursued and that your life is returned to you as best as we can make it after all these years. Your son asked that I move your daughter to the comfort of my chateau where she can rest until God chooses her fate. *That* is the decision I had to make, Erik. Thank God my son reminded me of who raised me. It is what my brother would have wanted. When God does choose, go. Go... and never return. My brother gave you the benefit of the doubt. I give you your freedom."

Anna's mouth gaped. Erik's eyes narrowed.

"What of Anna?" he asked. "What of her fate?"

"She won't have to worry over Belgium if that is what you ask," Raoul's voice lowered. "In all these years I've never had contact with the duke who allegedly wants her. Not once. Loup was hungry for her—and he is dead."

"This manhunt ends?" Erik asked.

Raoul nodded and caught a glimpse of Philippe. The boy's head tilted. It was as if he didn't comprehend.

"My answer to your request is yes," Raoul replied to his look. His eyes misted. "I will speak to the doctors."

"You weep for my daughter?" Erik asked incredulously.

"And for mine."

*"No, he is not a ghost; he is a man of
Heaven and earth, that is all."*
~Gaston Leroux, *The Phantom of the Opera*

TWENTY-THREE

There was a wind howling through the trees; a sound, which for as long as time stood was associated with Chagny. It was as familiar as the ivy that crawled up its walls and the fog that blanketed the lands on the warmer summer mornings. The ancient estate had seen its share of trials and triumphs. It housed visiting kings and exotic men from foreign nations. It laughed with holiday balls, celebrated weddings; it wept with decades of funerals.

But it had seen nothing like the time that had passed with a Phantom in its midst.

From the instant the caravan from Paris had arrived back at Chagny an estate once focused on obeying any order from France became an estate following any request from a Phantom.

Over several weeks the room that became Simone's was rarely without someone standing watch. The doctors came and went, bringing all sorts of oils and ointments. They tested treatments and strange looking liquids on the child, anything to wake the girl or bring down the fever that had set in. When Raoul stood watch, he'd bark orders to the servants who would scramble to obey his fervent commands for more cold towels or ice-water baths. Christine would enter and weep in the background still too heavy with guilt to offer much other than her prayers.

The time at Chagny tested Erik's limits of patience. Too many times he'd chastised himself for allowing Simone to taken from that hospital. But Erik knew a desperate situation when he saw one. In the end, like this son, he couldn't bear the idea of Simone waking in a cold hospital when there was a chance for her to wake where she may feel safe. She'd never survive a trip to Germany in her condition, and as much as he hated his baby girl inside the walls of Chagny, he loved his son. So to honor Philippe's wish for a sister he may lose, Erik gave in.

Keeping his focus on that to keep Erik in check. Nothing was redeeming about the weeks at Chagny other than Simone's comfort. Erik didn't trust these hallowed halls, or Raoul's intent to end the manhunt. But he did trust the vicomte's integrity, and for that reason, Erik lowered his guard about being in the home of his nemesis. The staff, though likely ordered not to fear a man in a mask or the child without one, apparently did. Erik suppressed his reactions and his ferocious need to protect Simone, realizing that it was better overall to the awkward atmosphere his family created in the household. André de Chagny was the spitting image of his uncle in deed and word. It made being treated like anyone else less strange. Erik made it a point to keep his family away from his noble hosts all he could, staying within the halls reserved for him and never straying far from Simone's side.

Erik was a genius, not a surgeon, so throughout the weeks, he allowed Raoul's doctors to use their potions and suspicious treatments to try to break Simone's fevers. When he'd had enough of their poking and prodding, he'd run them off, unwilling to see his baby girl suffer from one more needle prick or force-fed concoction. Sometimes, all he could do was let his stomach roll as he watched her thrash in feverous fits.

Simone didn't respond to any of it. Each time her eyes cracked open to milky white-slits, they'd flutter shut again. When she'd struggle to breathe, and Erik would hear Anna beg for her to speak, Erik would wish a thousand times to trade places with his little girl.

If she died, he'd may as well die with her.

Chickens clucked faintly in the distance, drawing Erik out of his thoughts. He barely heard them over Anna's tears the morning everything changed. They sounded as out of place at Chagny as Erik was. He looked up from Anna's shaking body and watery sobs and turned his emotion out the window. He let the pressure in his chest burst for the first time since he set foot in Chagny. His arms that had carried Simone through the doors felt weak as if their burden had been lifted. The chickens he stared at started to warp and blur. The birds had multiplied over the weeks from one flock to dozens. The vicomte and Philippe were at it in the courtyard again, adding more and more birds outside Simone's window in the hopes she would wake and hear them. It had been a ridiculous task for two boys desperate to feel like they had a magic cure.

A tear dripped from Erik's chin. His hand slid across Anna's shoulders as he left the room to deliver the news.

For the first time, the fog seemed out of place at Chagny. It was too early for it, but what did Raoul know about weather? He'd come to learn that nothing made much sense in life; especially the two figures he spied through his library window as they trudged through a light mist toward the Chagny crypts. Usually, the Chagny fog muffled the world and made it clean and quiet. Raoul wished it could have stifled his thoughts. Soon Chagny would be as it was but its occupants wouldn't. It would be years before Raoul would wake and not review everything that had come to pass. He sighed. Perhaps he had his own touch of madness, now.

"You are a million miles away."

Raoul abandoned his thoughts and glanced at his wife. She had lowered her needlepoint and shared his study of the scene out the window as well.

"I have a million things on my mind," he replied flatly.

"Like having Chagny back to normal?"

Chagny would never be normal again, and Raoul couldn't understand how she could say such a thing. They had changed. Significantly. He reached to the server at his side and removed the stopper from a crystal decanter. He stared at the cognac filling his glass but didn't have the humor to drink. It took him everything he had over the weeks to find ways to forgive Christine. The heart loves where it loves, and although she had tried to convince him that her heart was his, Raoul wasn't so sure. Trust, once lost, was hard to regain. He did his best though. It was all he could do. Raoul vowed his life to Christine, and his vow would remain as stable as Chagny's walls. As soon the carriage that stood loaded and waiting for its charges to depart Chagny, for good, he could breathe again.

Breathe, and start his marriage over.

"Like having you back," he whispered, though the words felt strained.

The weeks had been long for both them but time had a way of starting over with each coming dawn. Each morning he began by forgiving his wife and forgiving himself even with the presence of a Phantom among them. For the opportunity for grace, Raoul was thankful. He only regretted that such healing chances were spurred on at the bedside of a little girl who never should have been there, to begin with.

A knock scattered his thoughts. "Enter."

Raoul lowered the decanter as soon as he saw who entered. "Philippe." Raoul extended his hand toward him, while the lad bowed politely to his wife. The boy approached and shook it as if they were long friends. "I thought you would be readying to depart or with your parents," he gestured out the window.

Philippe looked in the direction of the crypt and sighed in a way that Raoul felt. "No. I wished to remain behind. To take my leave of André and Monsieur Legard." He smiled at Christine. "Your wife and I already spent a long time saying our goodbyes in the music room."

The music room saw a lot of those two, Raoul noted. The music that Raoul had learned Erik kept from Philippe, had become what the boy and his wife connected over. Hopefully,

Philippe would still have a chance to study music once he left Chagny. Raoul had come to respect his talent. He picked up his cognac and nodded. He shook the glass Philippe's way, but the boy declined.

"These last weeks have bonded you and our son in a way that reminds me much of my husband and his brother," Christine smiled as she lifted her needle and hoop again.

Raoul smiled at her but didn't feel it reach his eyes. It was the truth; he saw it too. "You regret leaving Chagny?" Raoul read sadness behind his eyes. Philippe nodded.

"I have found a sort of kindred spirits here, but my place is in Germany with my parents."

"Chagny will always be open to you," Christine assured. Raoul nodded in agreement.

"Thank you; you've been too kind," Philippe said. "I know it has been awkward having us here."

The silence told a story all its own.

"And you, Monsieur le Comte, are an honorable man." Philippe reached into his pocket and withdrew a small slip of paper from *L'Epoch*. He laid the cutting down on the server. "True to your word, this manhunt is over?"

Raoul lowered the cognac glass until it covered the small clipping and magnified the words beneath. Raoul laid his hand on Philippe's shoulder and looked on him with fatherly eyes. "It is, and God willing may we all move beyond it. I—" Overcome, Raoul stopped. "Son, I will never fully be amiable to your father. Some things will never be, and some histories never meant to be forgotten. But I can live where we are now with them forgiven— as my brother did."

Philippe nodded and stood quietly beside him for a long while. "I... I should go. The carriage is waiting, and we have a long trip back to Germany. Do you both mean it? Chagny will be open to me? I will see André again? See—Paris again?"

Raoul felt his eyes warm as Philippe extended his hand. His son had never had a friend as he did in Philippe. He still couldn't get over the idea that his vicomte's closest friend was the son of his greatest rival. The Lord worked in strange ways, and Raoul wasn't about to question the Lord. He took the lad's hand, noting its slight tremble, and drew the boy tightly into his embrace.

"You have my word," he whispered into his ear.

As Philippe released their embrace and glanced out the window, Raoul looked down and read the announcement on the clipping. He stood there simply to remain by the boy's side as long as he stared across Chagny, but knowing he stayed there to respect what the words meant to them all. The Persian had done as Raoul instructed. He closed his eyes and prayed those words would once and for all bring them all closure.

Erik and Anna are dead.

The wind blew the hem of Anna's skirt around her ankles making her draw the shawl tighter around her. The snow it grabbed danced in front of her before escaping on the breeze. Though she wanted to hasten to the carriage and be off to the seclusion of their monastery home—she let Erik take all the time he needed. He knelt before the crypt; his head bowed to the ground.

"Are you all right?" she asked softly.

"I am tired, Anna."

There was so much more than just physical exhaustion to that statement. Erik was speaking of life overall, and Anna felt it to her marrow. She blinked back tears. "We will be home soon."

"You are my home. I will be wherever you are." Erik struggled to his feet and laid a hand upon the name on the crypt. The gesture held more grief than time could cure. Anna curled her lips into her mouth and searched heaven for answers.

"This is over, Erik. The comte was true to his word. We need not ever associate ourselves with Chagny. You are free."

"We will always be associated with it." Erik traced the name. "And we are never entirely free of our pasts. We need its presence to learn how to shape our futures." Anna felt his reluctance as he turned from the crypt. "Come." He extended one hand to her and the other out to his opposite side. "Let us take our future home."

Anna smiled through her tears as Simone, sitting quietly by her father' side, took his hand and squealed as she was lifted high into his embrace. The violin she carried thumped lightly against Erik's back as they walked toward the awaiting carriage. Her bandages still peeked out from beneath her dress, but their presence didn't seem to dim her spirit or dull the rosy blush from her cheeks. The future held marvelous things the moment her fever broke, and Anna's sobs of joy had mingled in with clucking chickens. At that moment, choices were made to respect the past instead of resenting it.

"Papa!" Simone exclaimed, pointing back to the crypt with the bow.

Erik didn't turn. Anna stopped and looked behind to where Simone pointed, and for the first time tears of relief and peace ran down her face.

It was over—no more running. No more wondering if the past would haunt them. No more secrets between Chagny and a Phantom. Erik could live out his like anybody else, but she knew.

He would never be like anybody else.

Erik would always be the Phantom and a madman. Redemptions and cures were all contrary to the truth. He was not a man to be reformed or healed. He was merely a man who, imprisoned by a black and unpredictable madness, had a bright and supreme mind and a heart that could hold an empire. He knew what he needed to silence the noise and madness. He needed patience and extraordinary love. And now, by God's grace, that love kept jabbing him in the back with the bow.

"You forgot your package," Simone scolded.

"I didn't forget," Erik replied. "I've all the packages I need."

Anna smiled. Somehow she knew what he left wrapped in that parcel at the base of Philippe's crypt.

Paper. Ink. Figs.

About the Author

If one is going to query a publisher, Jennifer suggests not doing so in pink ink. Her first, written when she was twelve, was nothing if not colorful. Her passion lies in writing historical romances from forgotten pieces of history. In addition to her series expanding Leroux's *The Phantom of the Opera*, she writes romances set in the Regency and Victorian eras.

Jennifer admits to being country mouse with city mouse tastes and is constantly fighting to keep the little critters in line. She firmly believes organizations that support mental health awareness and her books often explore such challenges. She can't pronounce pistachio, hates lollipops with gooey centers, and thinks watermelon is the spawn of the devil. Most of all, she dearly loves to laugh. When not writing she can be found spending time leading her church small groups. Otherwise she spends time in the kitchen with her daughter, digging through antique stores for a quirky find, or entertaining the whims of her mischievous pug.

Turns out, the pug has her well trained.

The Phantom Series
Jennifer Deschanel

Desired by the Phantom
Pursued by the Phantom
Captured by the Phantom

Made in United States
Orlando, FL
14 December 2023

40915746R00124